TOP SECRET GRAPHICA MYSTERIES

CASEBOOK: WEREWOLVES

WITHDRAWN

Script by Justine and Ron Fontes

Layouts and Designs by Ron Fontes

Skyview Books™

an imprint of
WINDMILL BOOKS™
New York

Published in 2010 by Windmill Books, LLC
303 Park Avenue South, Suite # 1280
New York, NY 10010-3657

CREDITS:
Script by Justine and Ron Fontes
Layouts and designs by Ron Fontes
Art by Planman, Ltd.

Publisher Cataloging in Publication

Fontes, Justine
     Casebook—Werewolves. – School and library ed. / script by Justine and Ron Fontes ; layouts and designs by Ron Fontes.
     p.   cm. – (Top secret graphica mysteries)
Summary: When Einstein and his friends from the Windmill Bakery use their virtual visors to investigate legends of werewolves, they are joined by Mike, Clarita's cousin, who thinks he is a werewolf.
ISBN 978-1-60754-609-2. – ISBN 978-1-60754-611-5 (pbk.)
ISBN 978-1-60754-610-8 (6-pack)
     1. Werewolves—Juvenile fiction   2. Graphic novels [1. Werewolves—Fiction   2. Graphic novels] I. Fontes, Ron   II. Title   III. Title: Werewolves
IV. Series
     741.5/973—dc22

Manufactured in the United States of America

CPSIA Compliance Information: Batch #BW10W: For futher information contact Windmill Books, New York, New York at 1-866-478-0556.

CONTENTS

Welcome to the Windmill Bakery

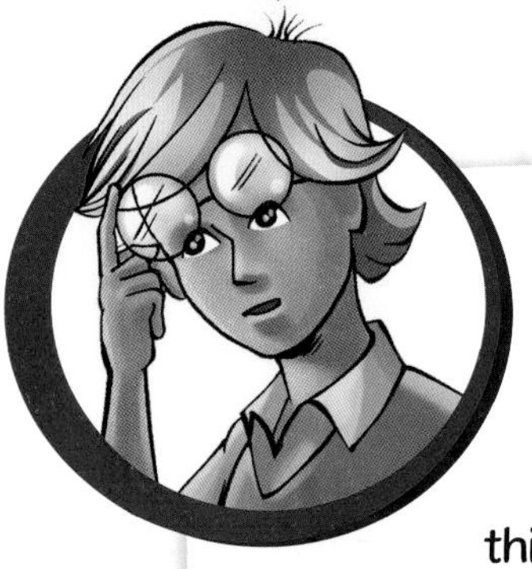

Edward Icarus Stein is known as "Einstein" because of his initials "E.I." and his last name, and because he loves science the way fanatical fans love sports. Einstein dedicates his waking hours to observing as much as he can of all the strange things just beyond human knowledge, because "that's the discovery zone," as he calls it. Einstein aspires to nothing less than living up to his nickname and coming up with a truly groundbreaking scientific discovery. So far this brilliant seventh grader's best invention is the Virtual Visors he and his friends use to explore strange phenomena. Einstein's parents own the local bakery where the friends meet.

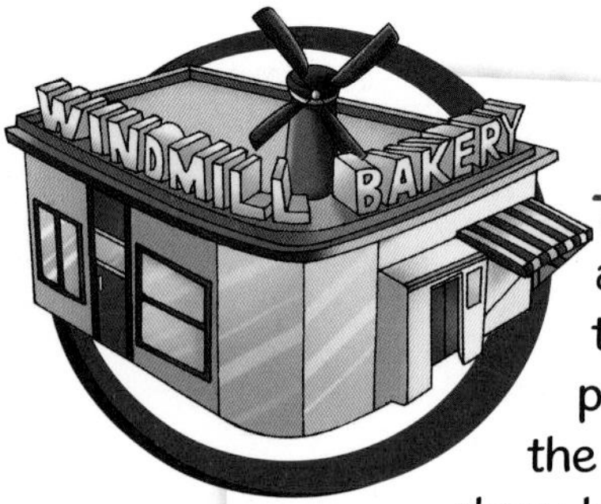
WINDMILL BAKERY

The Windmill Bakery is a cozy place where friends and neighbors buy homemade goodies to go or to eat on the premises. Einstein's kindhearted parents make everyone feel welcome, especially the friends who understand their exceptional son and share his appetite for discovery!

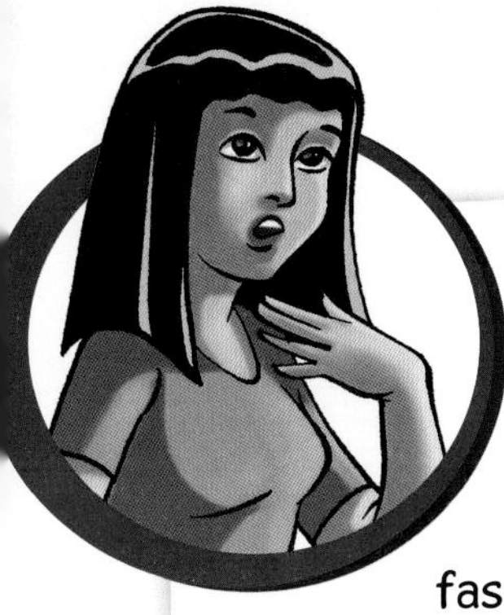

"Spacey Tracy" Lee saw a UFO when she was seven. Her parents tried to dismiss the incident as a "waking dream." But Tracy knew what she saw and it inspired her to investigate the UFO phenomenon. The more she learned, the more fascinated she became. She earned her nickname by constantly talking about UFOs. Tracy hopes to become a reporter when she grows up so she can continue to explore the unknown. A straight-A student, Tracy enjoys swimming, gymnastics, and playing the cello. Now that she's "more mature" and hoping to lose the silly nickname, Tracy shares the experience that changed her life forever only with her Virtual Visor buddies.

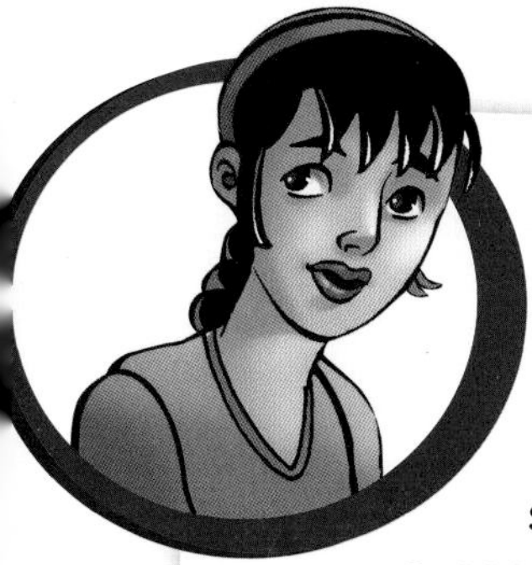

Clarita Gonzales knows that Indiana Jones and Lara Croft aren't real people, but that doesn't stop this seventh grader from wanting to be an adventurous archaeologist. Clarita's parents will support any path she chooses, as long as she gets a good education. Unfortunately, school isn't her strong point. During most classes, Clarita's mind wanders to, as she puts it, "more exciting places—like Atlantis!" A tomboy thanks to her three older brothers and one younger brother, Clarita is a great soccer player and is also into martial arts. Her interest in archaeology extends to architecture, artifacts, cooking, and all forms of culture. (Clarita would have a crush on Einstein if he wasn't "such a bookworm")!

"Freaky Frank" Phillips earned his nickname because of his uncanny ability to use his "extra senses," a "gift" he inherited from his grandma. Though this eighth grader can't predict the winners of the next SUPERBOWL (or, he admits, "anything really useful"), Frank "knows" when someone is lying or otherwise up to no good. He gets "warnings" before trouble strikes. And sometimes he "sees things that aren't there"—at least to those less sensitive to things like auras and ghosts. Frank isn't sure what he wants to be when he grows up. He enjoys keeping tropical fish and does well in every subject, except math. "Numbers make my head hurt," Frank confesses. Frank spends lots of time with his family and his fish, but he's always up for an adventure with his friends.

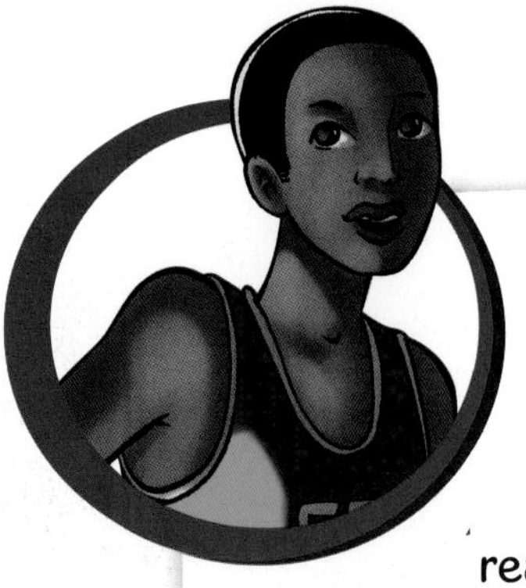

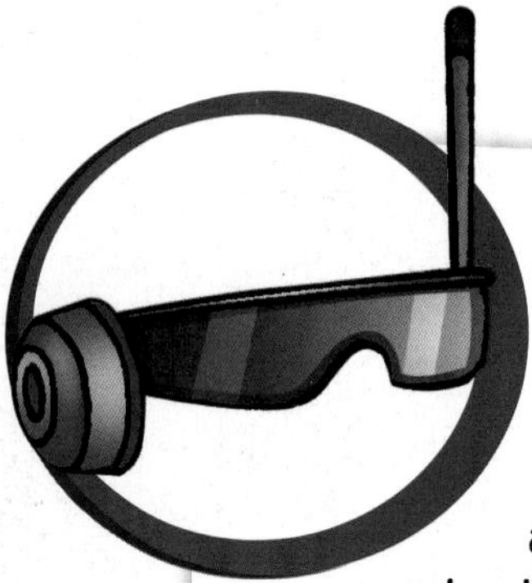

The Virtual Visors allow Einstein, Frank, Clarita, and Tracy to pursue their taste for adventure well beyond the boundaries of the bakery. Thanks to Einstein's brilliant software, the visors can simulate all kinds of locations and experiences based on the uploaded facts. Once inside the program, the visors become invisible. When danger gets too intense, the kids can always touch their Virtual Visors to return to the bakery. Sometimes the kids explore in the real world without the visors. But more often they use these devices to explore the mysteries and phenomena that intrigue each member of the group. The Virtual Visors are the ultimate virtual reality research tool, even though you never know what quirky things might happen thanks to Einstein's "Random Adventure Program."

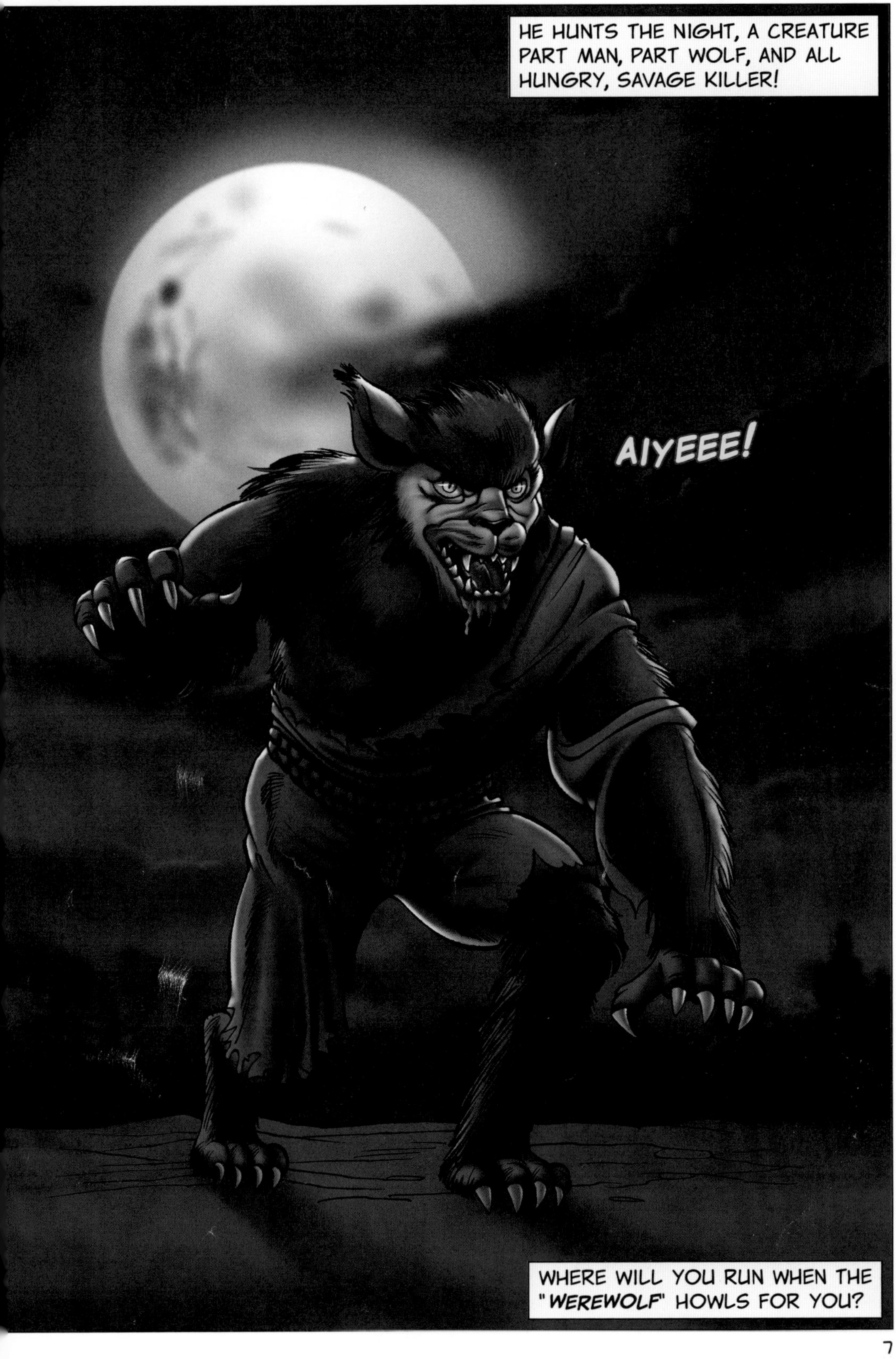
HE HUNTS THE NIGHT, A CREATURE PART MAN, PART WOLF, AND ALL HUNGRY, SAVAGE KILLER!
AIYEEE!
WHERE WILL YOU RUN WHEN THE "WEREWOLF" HOWLS FOR YOU?

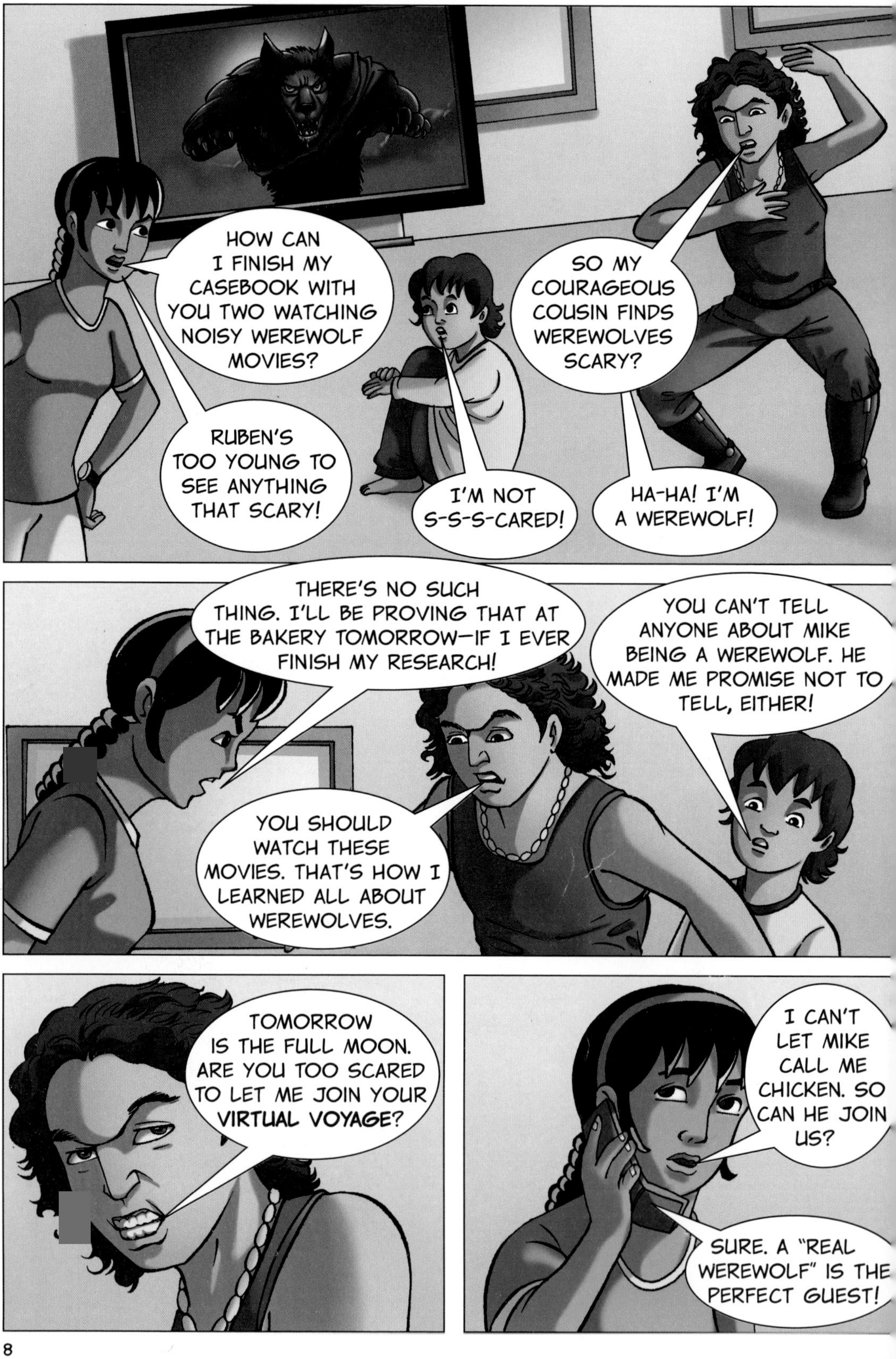
HOW CAN I FINISH MY CASEBOOK WITH YOU TWO WATCHING NOISY WEREWOLF MOVIES?
RUBEN'S TOO YOUNG TO SEE ANYTHING THAT SCARY!
I'M NOT S-S-S-CARED!
SO MY COURAGEOUS COUSIN FINDS WEREWOLVES SCARY?
HA-HA! I'M A WEREWOLF!
THERE'S NO SUCH THING. I'LL BE PROVING THAT AT THE BAKERY TOMORROW—IF I EVER FINISH MY RESEARCH!
YOU SHOULD WATCH THESE MOVIES. THAT'S HOW I LEARNED ALL ABOUT WEREWOLVES.
YOU CAN'T TELL ANYONE ABOUT MIKE BEING A WEREWOLF. HE MADE ME PROMISE NOT TO TELL, EITHER!
TOMORROW IS THE FULL MOON. ARE YOU TOO SCARED TO LET ME JOIN YOUR VIRTUAL VOYAGE?
I CAN'T LET MIKE CALL ME CHICKEN. SO CAN HE JOIN US?
SURE. A "REAL WEREWOLF" IS THE PERFECT GUEST!

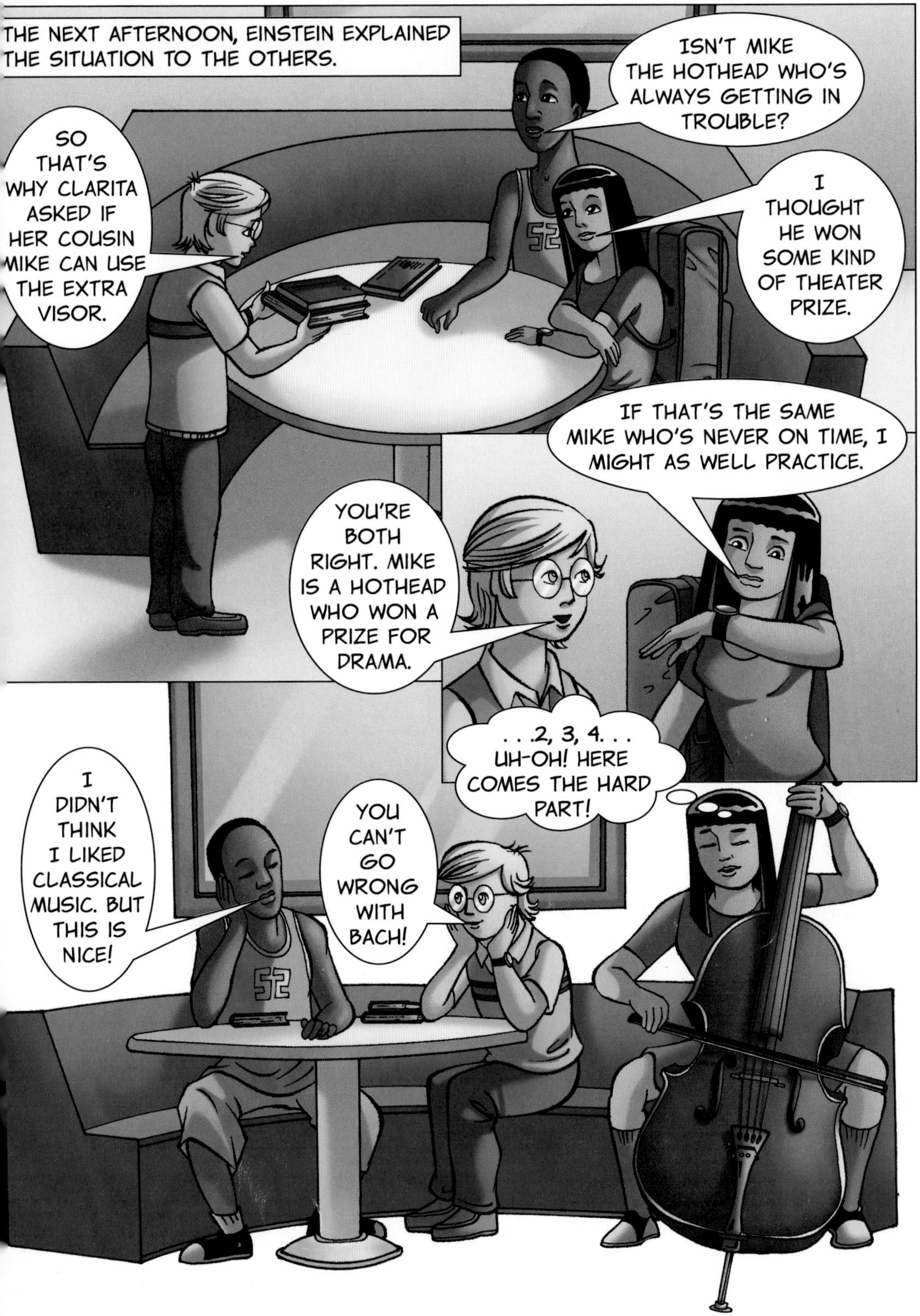
THE NEXT AFTERNOON, EINSTEIN EXPLAINED THE SITUATION TO THE OTHERS.
ISN'T MIKE THE HOTHEAD WHO'S ALWAYS GETTING IN TROUBLE?
SO THAT'S WHY CLARITA ASKED IF HER COUSIN MIKE CAN USE THE EXTRA VISOR.
I THOUGHT HE WON SOME KIND OF THEATER PRIZE.
IF THAT'S THE SAME MIKE WHO'S NEVER ON TIME, I MIGHT AS WELL PRACTICE.
YOU'RE BOTH RIGHT. MIKE IS A HOTHEAD WHO WON A PRIZE FOR DRAMA.
. . .2, 3, 4. . . UH-OH! HERE COMES THE HARD PART!
I DIDN'T THINK I LIKED CLASSICAL MUSIC. BUT THIS IS NICE!
YOU CAN'T GO WRONG WITH BACH!

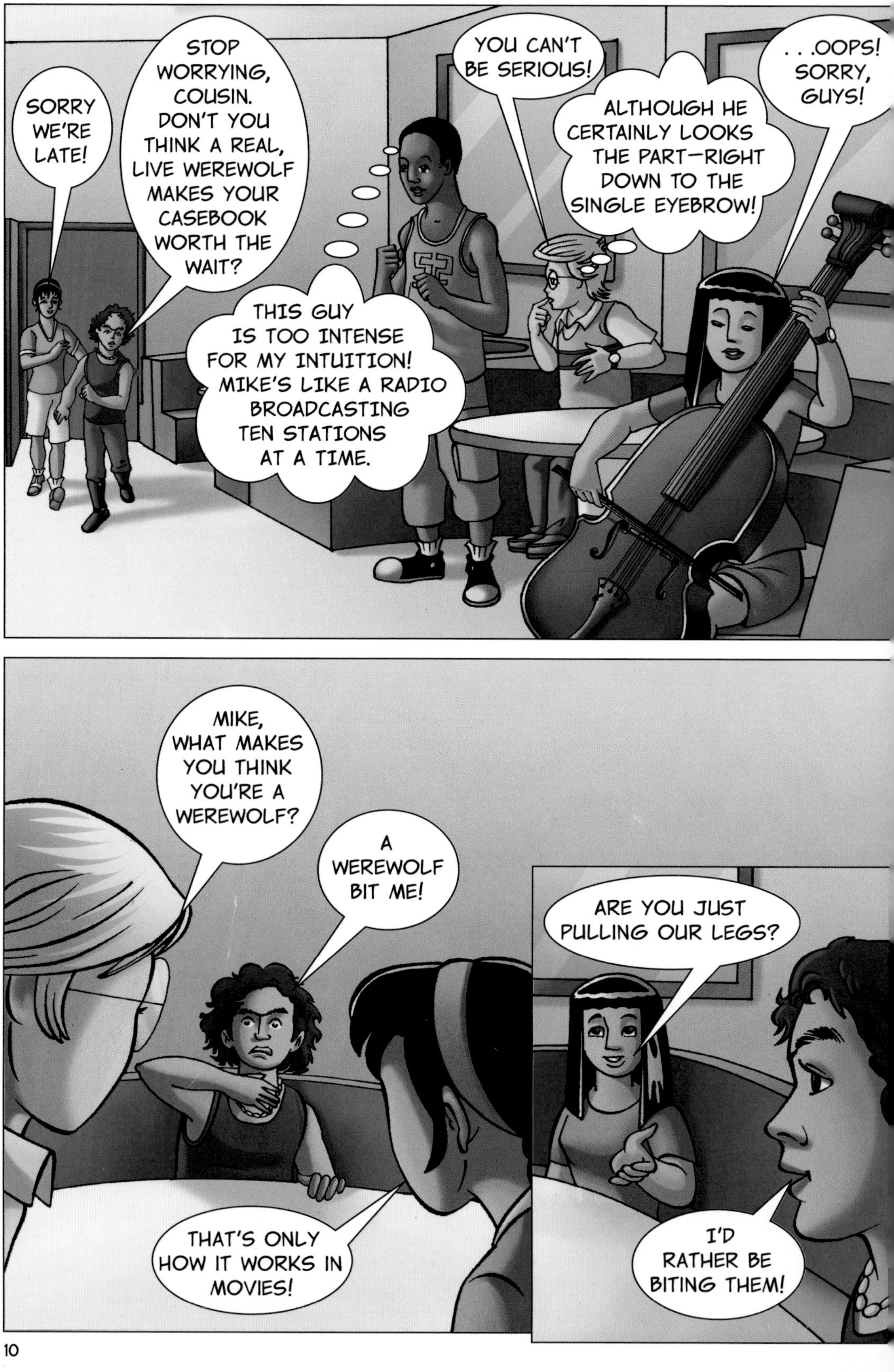
SORRY WE'RE LATE!
STOP WORRYING, COUSIN. DON'T YOU THINK A REAL, LIVE WEREWOLF MAKES YOUR CASEBOOK WORTH THE WAIT?
THIS GUY IS TOO INTENSE FOR MY INTUITION! MIKE'S LIKE A RADIO BROADCASTING TEN STATIONS AT A TIME.
YOU CAN'T BE SERIOUS!
ALTHOUGH HE CERTAINLY LOOKS THE PART—RIGHT DOWN TO THE SINGLE EYEBROW!
. . .OOPS! SORRY, GUYS!
MIKE, WHAT MAKES YOU THINK YOU'RE A WEREWOLF?
A WEREWOLF BIT ME!
THAT'S ONLY HOW IT WORKS IN MOVIES!
ARE YOU JUST PULLING OUR LEGS?
I'D RATHER BE BITING THEM!

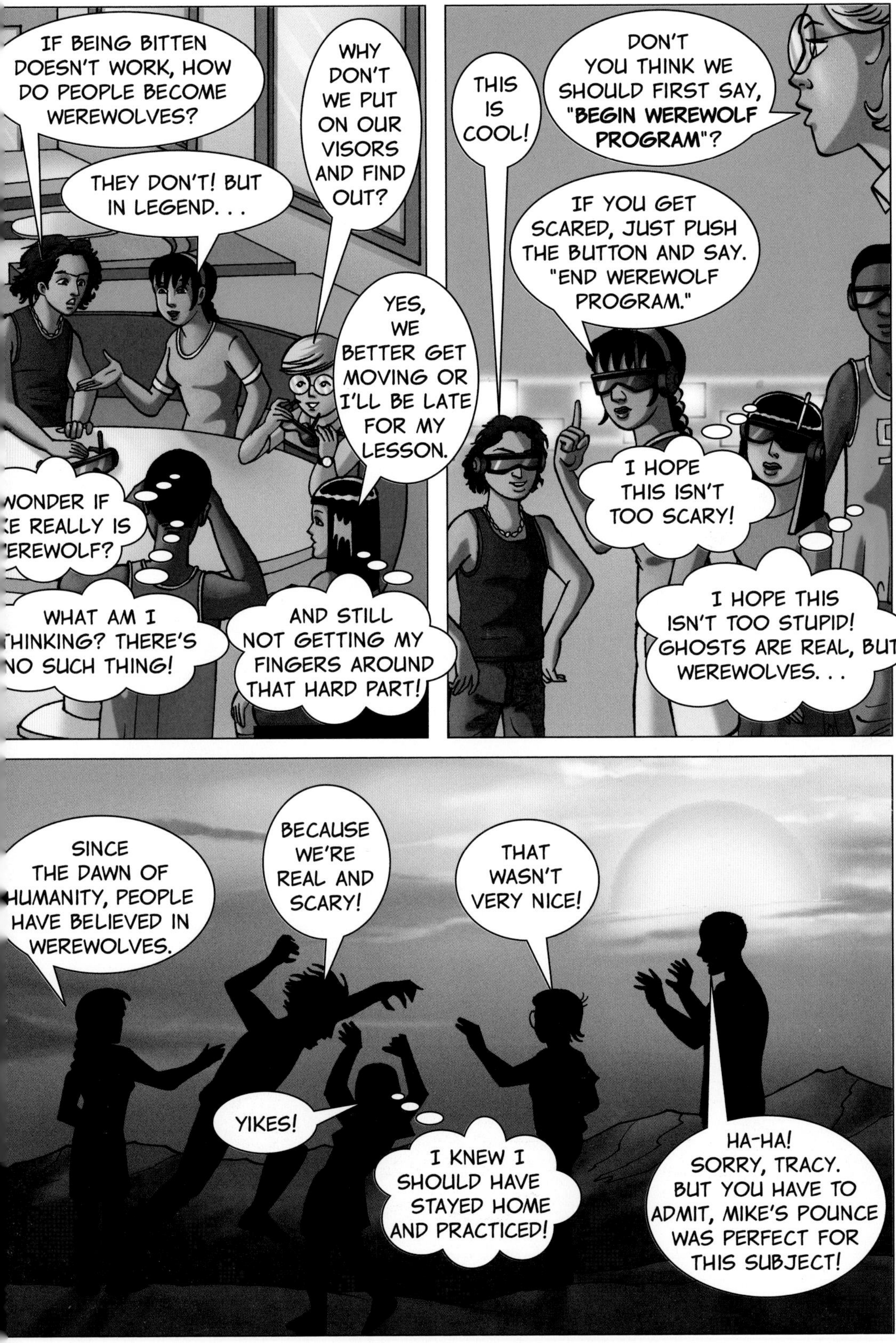
IF BEING BITTEN DOESN'T WORK, HOW DO PEOPLE BECOME WEREWOLVES?
THEY DON'T! BUT IN LEGEND. . .
WHY DON'T WE PUT ON OUR VISORS AND FIND OUT?
YES, WE BETTER GET MOVING OR I'LL BE LATE FOR MY LESSON.
WONDER IF E REALLY IS EREWOLF?
WHAT AM I HINKING? THERE'S NO SUCH THING!
AND STILL NOT GETTING MY FINGERS AROUND THAT HARD PART!
THIS IS COOL!
DON'T YOU THINK WE SHOULD FIRST SAY, "**BEGIN WEREWOLF PROGRAM**"?
IF YOU GET SCARED, JUST PUSH THE BUTTON AND SAY. "END WEREWOLF PROGRAM."
I HOPE THIS ISN'T TOO SCARY!
I HOPE THIS ISN'T TOO STUPID! GHOSTS ARE REAL, BUT WEREWOLVES. . .
SINCE THE DAWN OF HUMANITY, PEOPLE HAVE BELIEVED IN WEREWOLVES.
BECAUSE WE'RE REAL AND SCARY!
THAT WASN'T VERY NICE!
YIKES!
I KNEW I SHOULD HAVE STAYED HOME AND PRACTICED!
HA-HA! SORRY, TRACY. BUT YOU HAVE TO ADMIT, MIKE'S POUNCE WAS PERFECT FOR THIS SUBJECT!

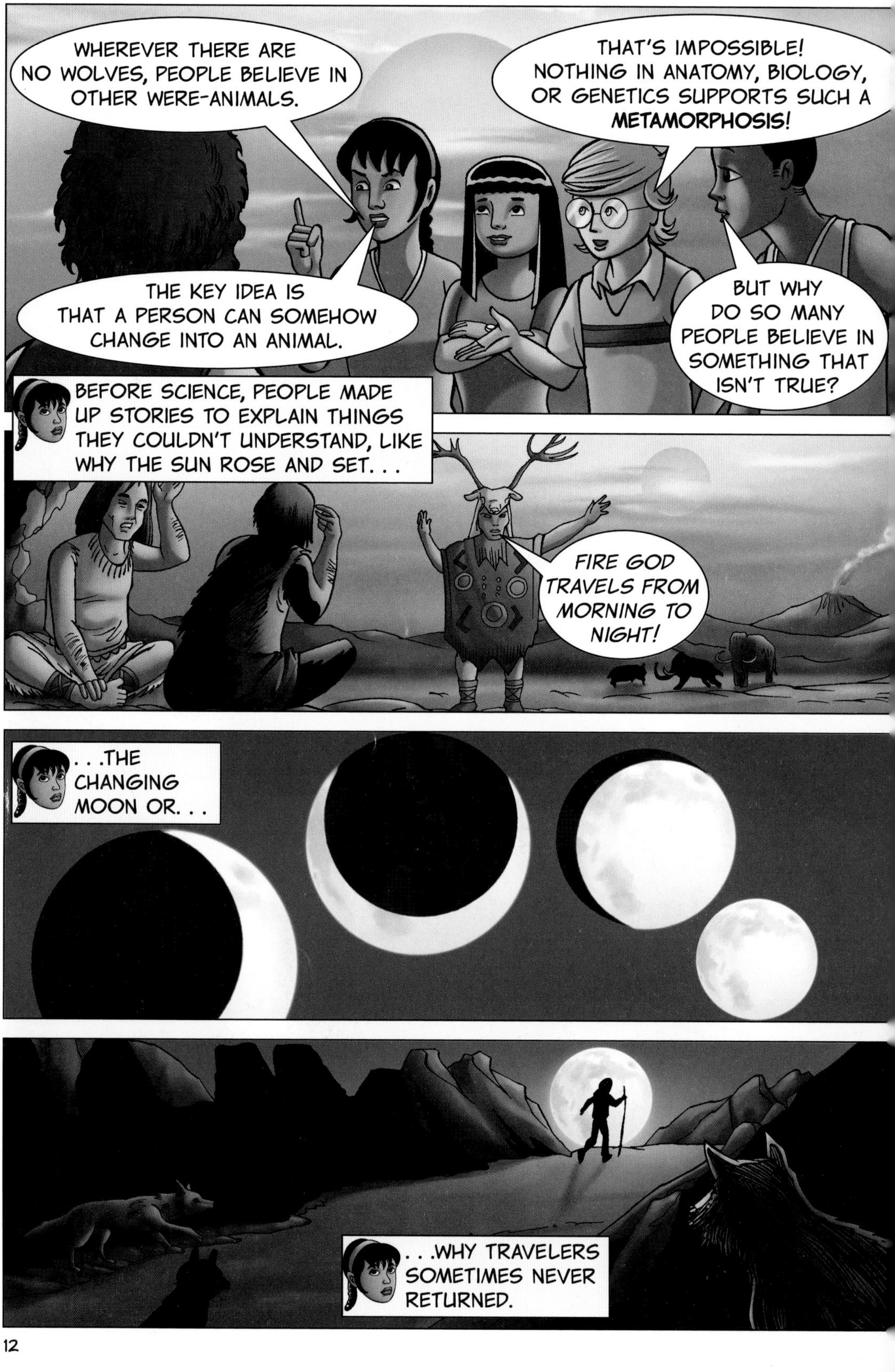
WHEREVER THERE ARE NO WOLVES, PEOPLE BELIEVE IN OTHER WERE-ANIMALS.
THAT'S IMPOSSIBLE! NOTHING IN ANATOMY, BIOLOGY, OR GENETICS SUPPORTS SUCH A **METAMORPHOSIS**!
THE KEY IDEA IS THAT A PERSON CAN SOMEHOW CHANGE INTO AN ANIMAL.
BUT WHY DO SO MANY PEOPLE BELIEVE IN SOMETHING THAT ISN'T TRUE?
BEFORE SCIENCE, PEOPLE MADE UP STORIES TO EXPLAIN THINGS THEY COULDN'T UNDERSTAND, LIKE WHY THE SUN ROSE AND SET. . .
FIRE GOD TRAVELS FROM MORNING TO NIGHT!
. . .THE CHANGING MOON OR. . .
. . .WHY TRAVELERS SOMETIMES NEVER RETURNED.

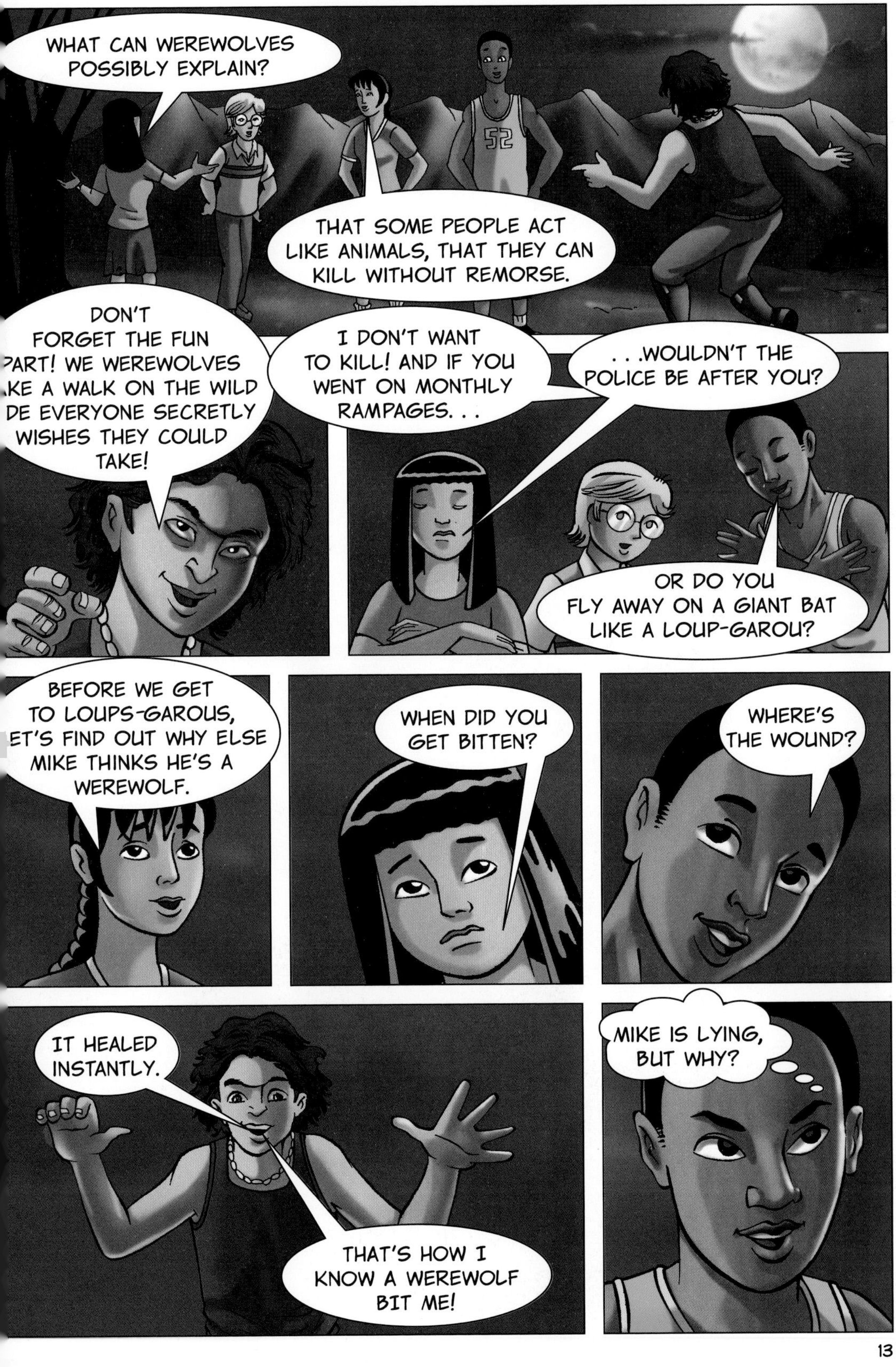
WHAT CAN WEREWOLVES POSSIBLY EXPLAIN?
THAT SOME PEOPLE ACT LIKE ANIMALS, THAT THEY CAN KILL WITHOUT REMORSE.
DON'T FORGET THE FUN ART! WE WEREWOLVES KE A WALK ON THE WILD DE EVERYONE SECRETLY WISHES THEY COULD TAKE!
I DON'T WANT TO KILL! AND IF YOU WENT ON MONTHLY RAMPAGES. . .
. . .WOULDN'T THE POLICE BE AFTER YOU?
OR DO YOU FLY AWAY ON A GIANT BAT LIKE A LOUP-GAROU?
BEFORE WE GET TO LOUPS-GAROUS, ET'S FIND OUT WHY ELSE MIKE THINKS HE'S A WEREWOLF.
WHEN DID YOU GET BITTEN?
WHERE'S THE WOUND?
IT HEALED INSTANTLY.
THAT'S HOW I KNOW A WEREWOLF BIT ME!
MIKE IS LYING, BUT WHY?

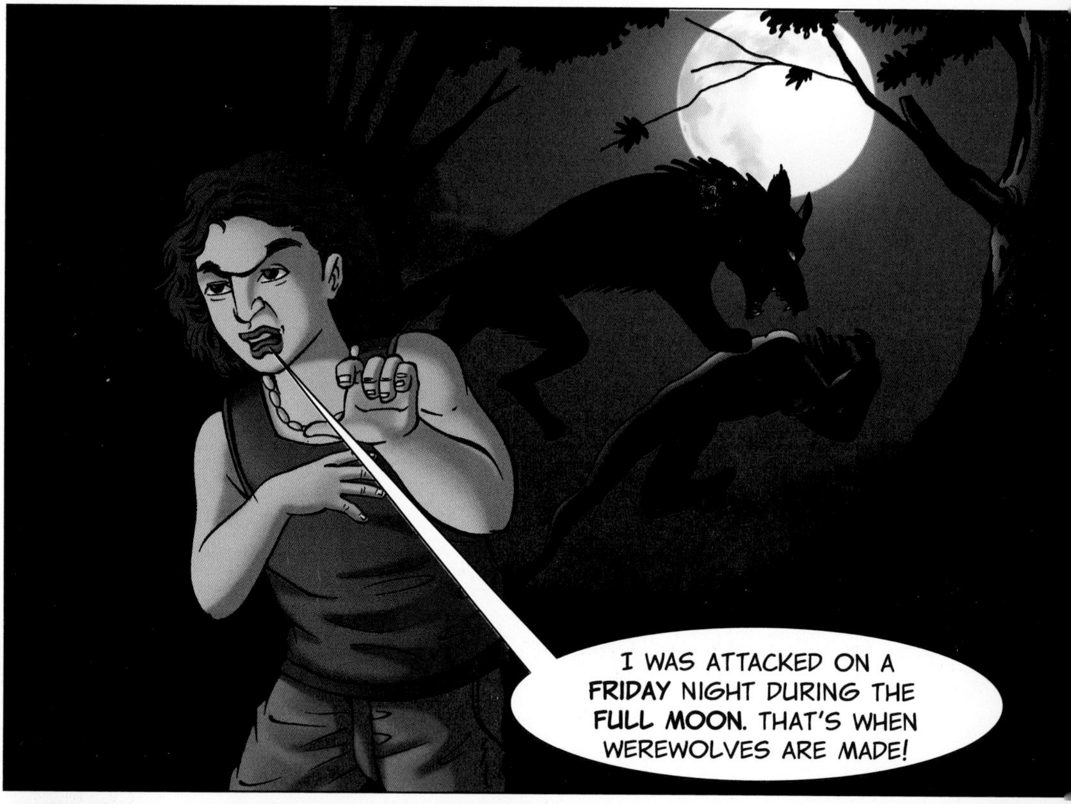
I WAS ATTACKED ON A **FRIDAY** NIGHT DURING THE **FULL MOON.** THAT'S WHEN WEREWOLVES ARE MADE!

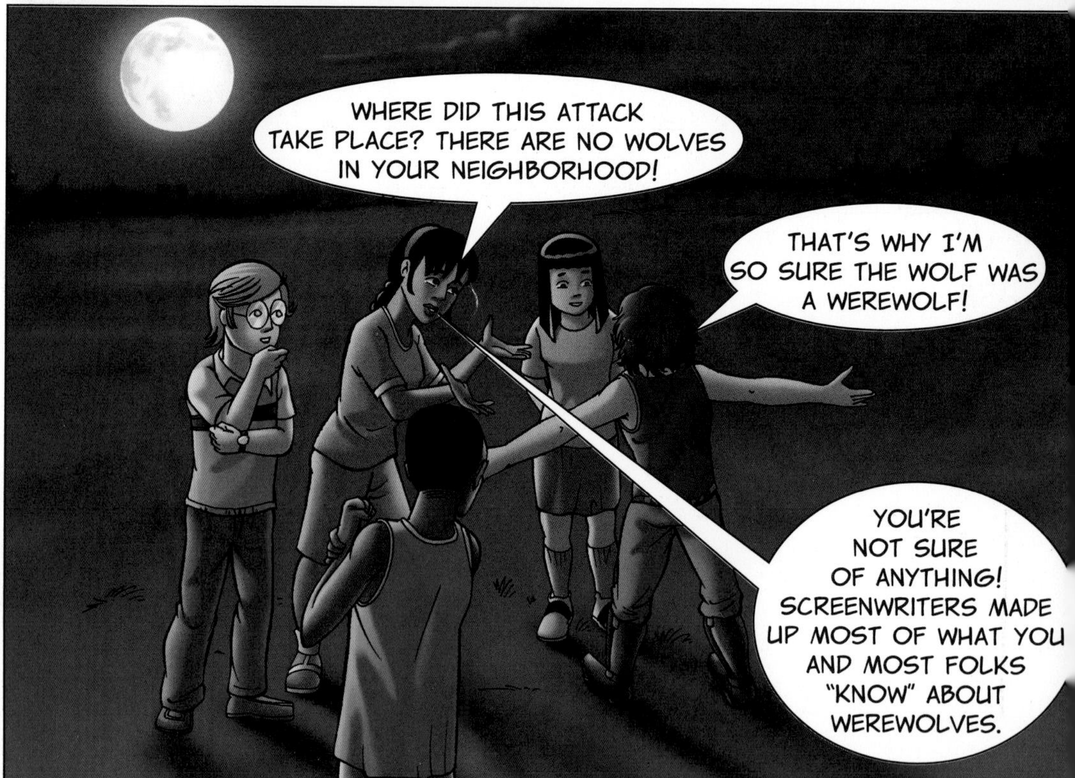
WHERE DID THIS ATTACK TAKE PLACE? THERE ARE NO WOLVES IN YOUR NEIGHBORHOOD!
THAT'S WHY I'M SO SURE THE WOLF WAS A WEREWOLF!
YOU'RE NOT SURE OF ANYTHING! SCREENWRITERS MADE UP MOST OF WHAT YOU AND MOST FOLKS "KNOW" ABOUT WEREWOLVES.

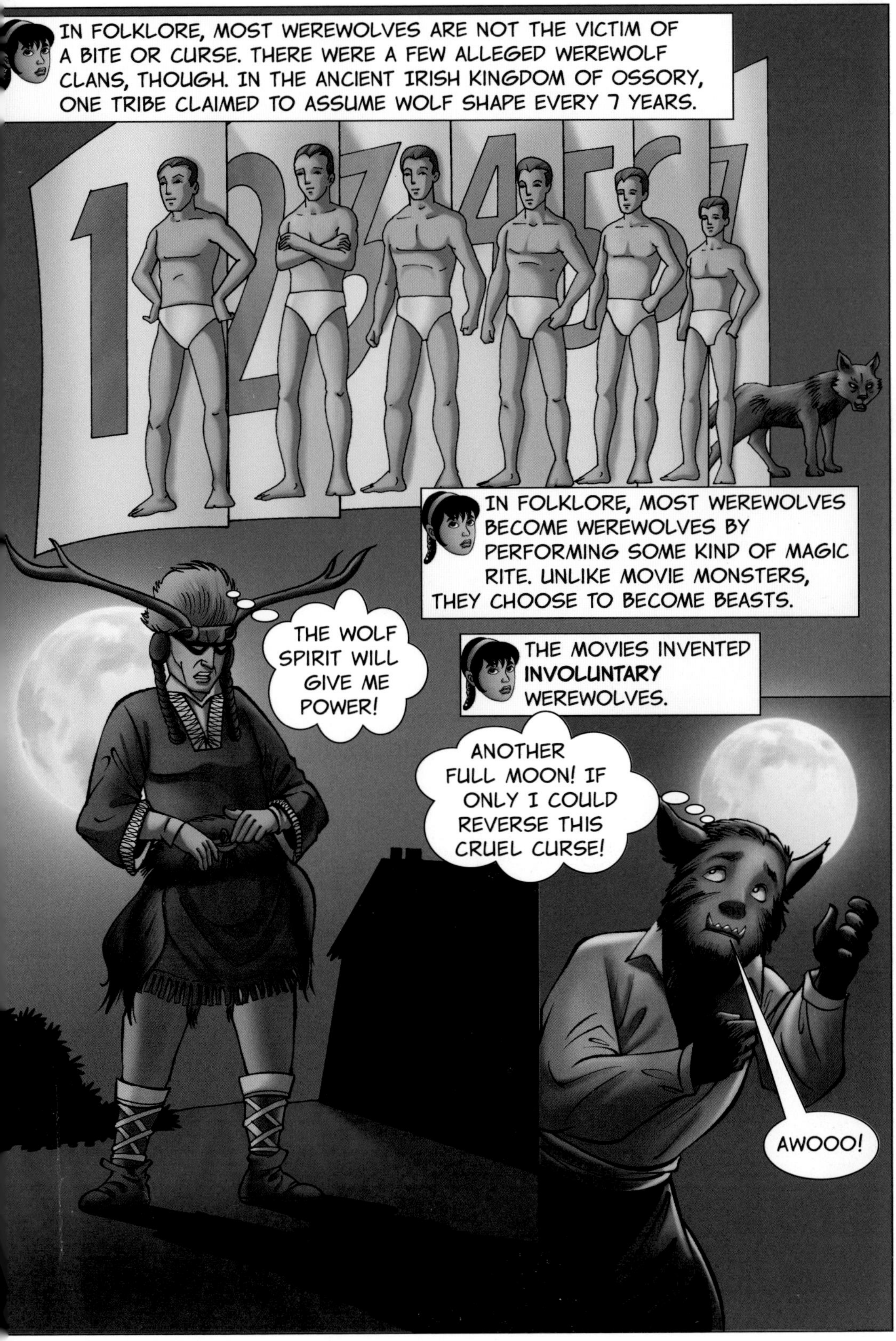
IN FOLKLORE, MOST WEREWOLVES ARE NOT THE VICTIM OF A BITE OR CURSE. THERE WERE A FEW ALLEGED WEREWOLF CLANS, THOUGH. IN THE ANCIENT IRISH KINGDOM OF OSSORY, ONE TRIBE CLAIMED TO ASSUME WOLF SHAPE EVERY 7 YEARS.
IN FOLKLORE, MOST WEREWOLVES BECOME WEREWOLVES BY PERFORMING SOME KIND OF MAGIC RITE. UNLIKE MOVIE MONSTERS, THEY CHOOSE TO BECOME BEASTS.
THE WOLF SPIRIT WILL GIVE ME POWER!
THE MOVIES INVENTED **INVOLUNTARY** WEREWOLVES.
ANOTHER FULL MOON! IF ONLY I COULD REVERSE THIS CRUEL CURSE!
AWOOO!

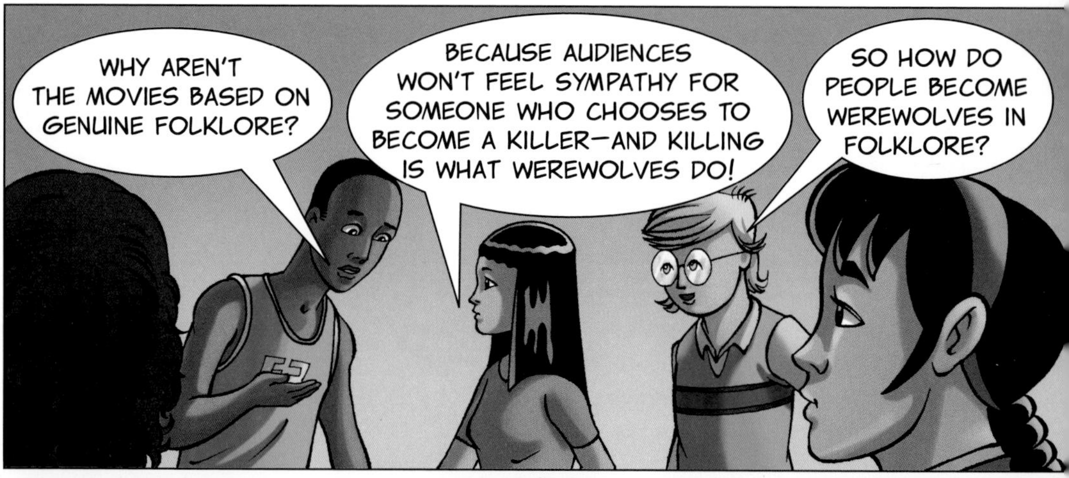
WHY AREN'T THE MOVIES BASED ON GENUINE FOLKLORE?
BECAUSE AUDIENCES WON'T FEEL SYMPATHY FOR SOMEONE WHO CHOOSES TO BECOME A KILLER—AND KILLING IS WHAT WEREWOLVES DO!
SO HOW DO PEOPLE BECOME WEREWOLVES IN FOLKLORE?

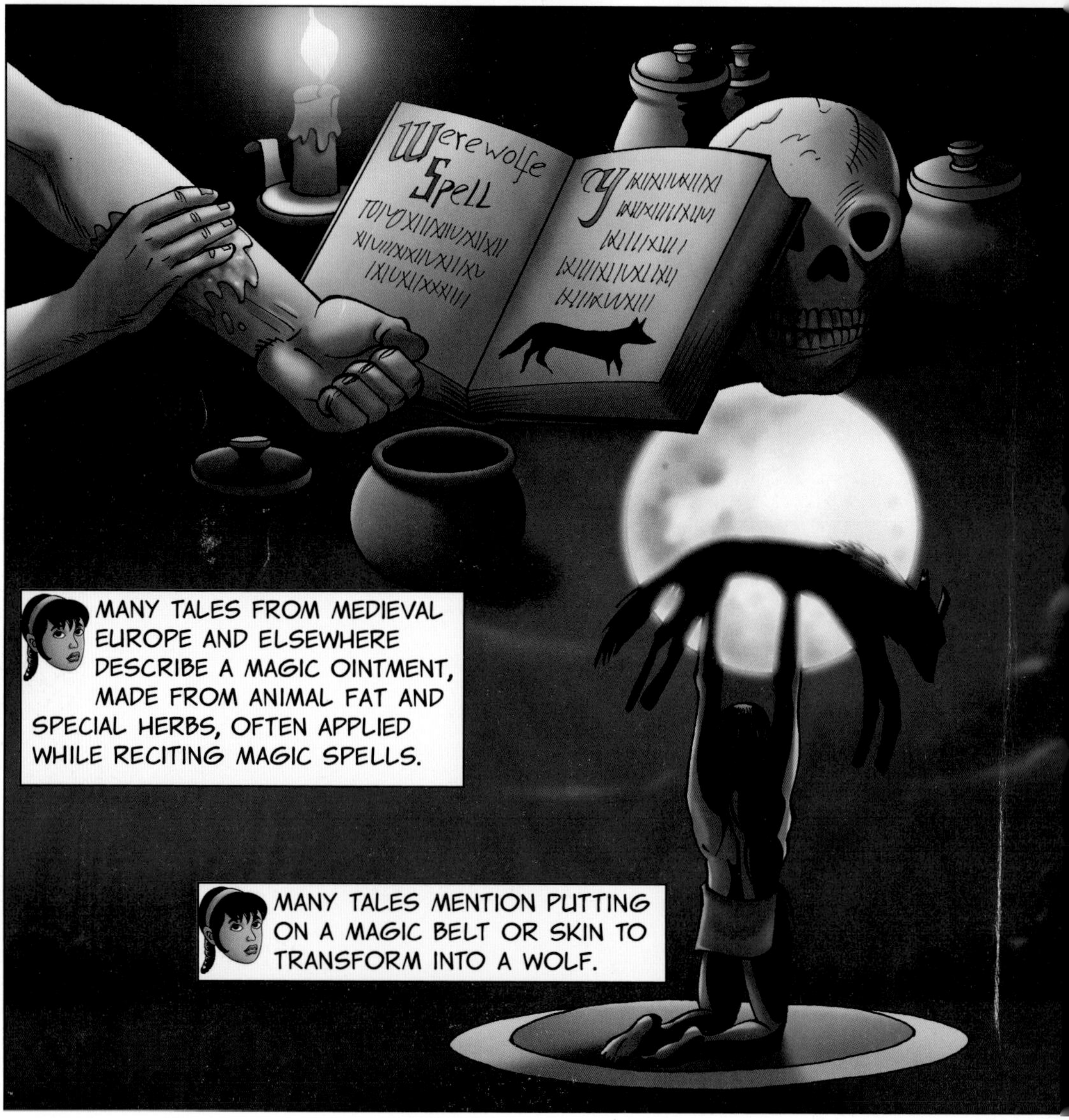
Werewolfe Spell
MANY TALES FROM MEDIEVAL EUROPE AND ELSEWHERE DESCRIBE A MAGIC OINTMENT, MADE FROM ANIMAL FAT AND SPECIAL HERBS, OFTEN APPLIED WHILE RECITING MAGIC SPELLS.
MANY TALES MENTION PUTTING ON A MAGIC BELT OR SKIN TO TRANSFORM INTO A WOLF.

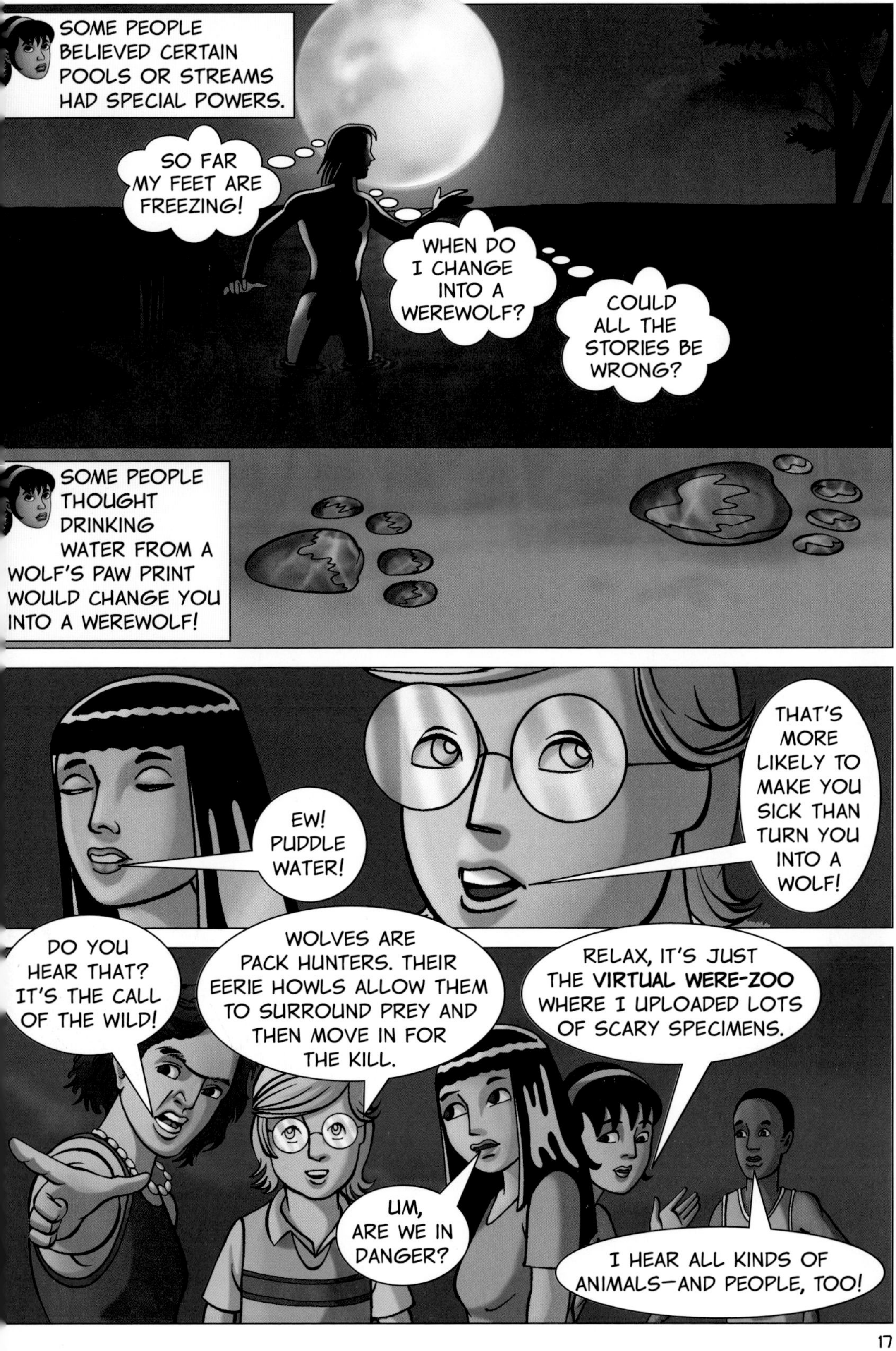
SOME PEOPLE BELIEVED CERTAIN POOLS OR STREAMS HAD SPECIAL POWERS.
SO FAR MY FEET ARE FREEZING!
WHEN DO I CHANGE INTO A WEREWOLF?
COULD ALL THE STORIES BE WRONG?
SOME PEOPLE THOUGHT DRINKING WATER FROM A WOLF'S PAW PRINT WOULD CHANGE YOU INTO A WEREWOLF!
EW! PUDDLE WATER!
THAT'S MORE LIKELY TO MAKE YOU SICK THAN TURN YOU INTO A WOLF!
DO YOU HEAR THAT? IT'S THE CALL OF THE WILD!
WOLVES ARE PACK HUNTERS. THEIR EERIE HOWLS ALLOW THEM TO SURROUND PREY AND THEN MOVE IN FOR THE KILL.
RELAX, IT'S JUST THE **VIRTUAL WERE-ZOO** WHERE I UPLOADED LOTS OF SCARY SPECIMENS.
UM, ARE WE IN DANGER?
I HEAR ALL KINDS OF ANIMALS—AND PEOPLE, TOO!

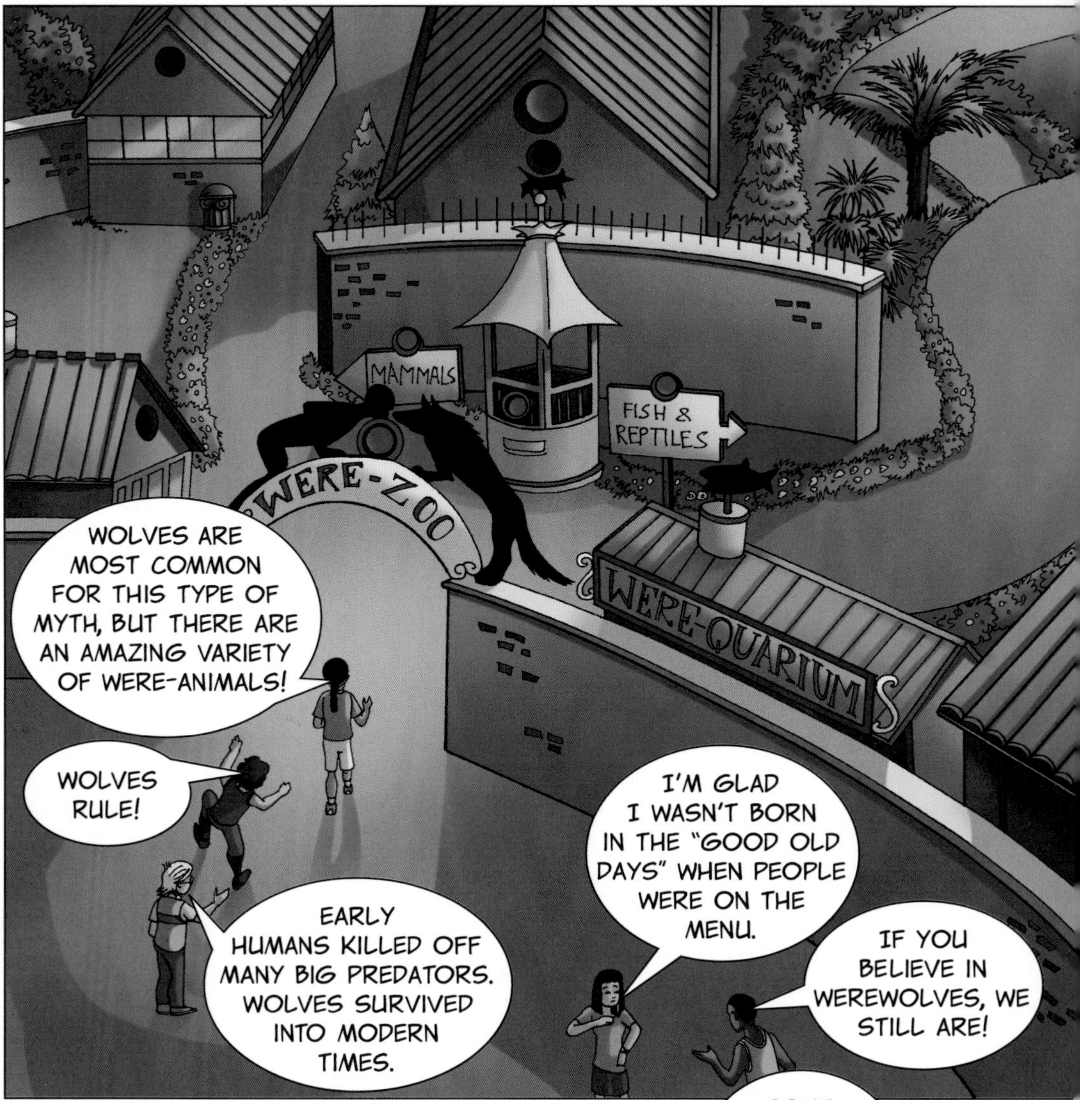
MAMMALS
FISH & REPTILES
WERE-ZOO
WERE-QUARIUM
WOLVES ARE MOST COMMON FOR THIS TYPE OF MYTH, BUT THERE ARE AN AMAZING VARIETY OF WERE-ANIMALS!
WOLVES RULE!
EARLY HUMANS KILLED OFF MANY BIG PREDATORS. WOLVES SURVIVED INTO MODERN TIMES.
I'M GLAD I WASN'T BORN IN THE "GOOD OLD DAYS" WHEN PEOPLE WERE ON THE MENU.
IF YOU BELIEVE IN WEREWOLVES, WE STILL ARE!

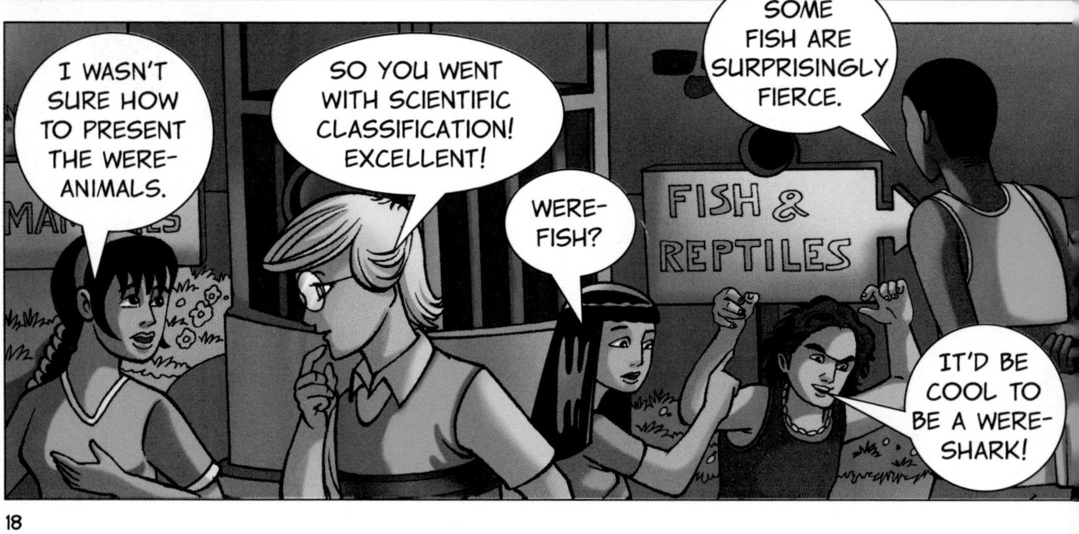
I WASN'T SURE HOW TO PRESENT THE WERE-ANIMALS.
SO YOU WENT WITH SCIENTIFIC CLASSIFICATION! EXCELLENT!
WERE-FISH?
SOME FISH ARE SURPRISINGLY FIERCE.
FISH & REPTILES
IT'D BE COOL TO BE A WERE-SHARK!

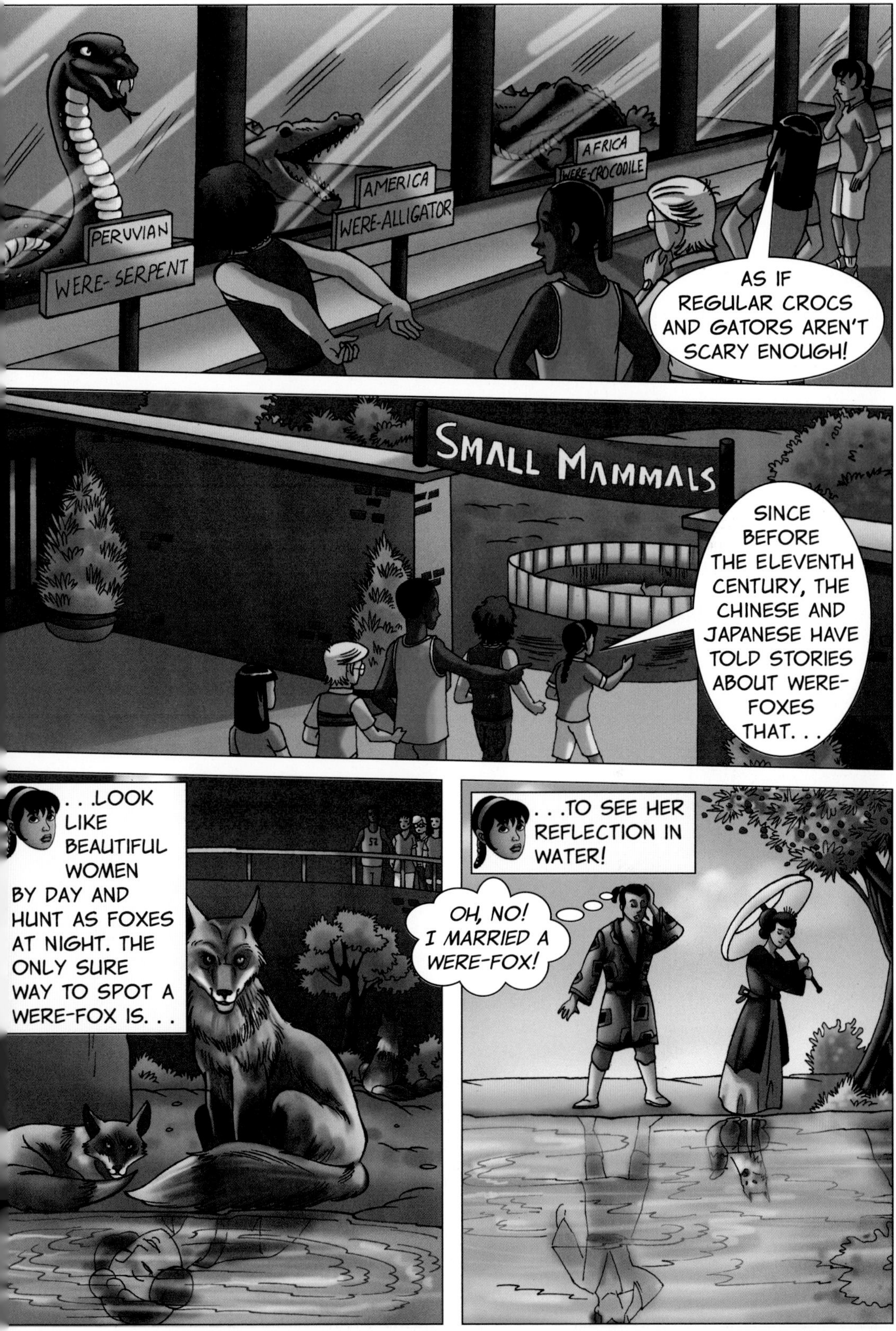
PERUVIAN
WERE-SERPENT
AMERICA
WERE-ALLIGATOR
AFRICA
WERE-CROCODILE
AS IF REGULAR CROCS AND GATORS AREN'T SCARY ENOUGH!
SMALL MAMMALS
SINCE BEFORE THE ELEVENTH CENTURY, THE CHINESE AND JAPANESE HAVE TOLD STORIES ABOUT WERE-FOXES THAT. . .
. . .LOOK LIKE BEAUTIFUL WOMEN BY DAY AND HUNT AS FOXES AT NIGHT. THE ONLY SURE WAY TO SPOT A WERE-FOX IS. . .
. . .TO SEE HER REFLECTION IN WATER!
OH, NO! I MARRIED A WERE-FOX!

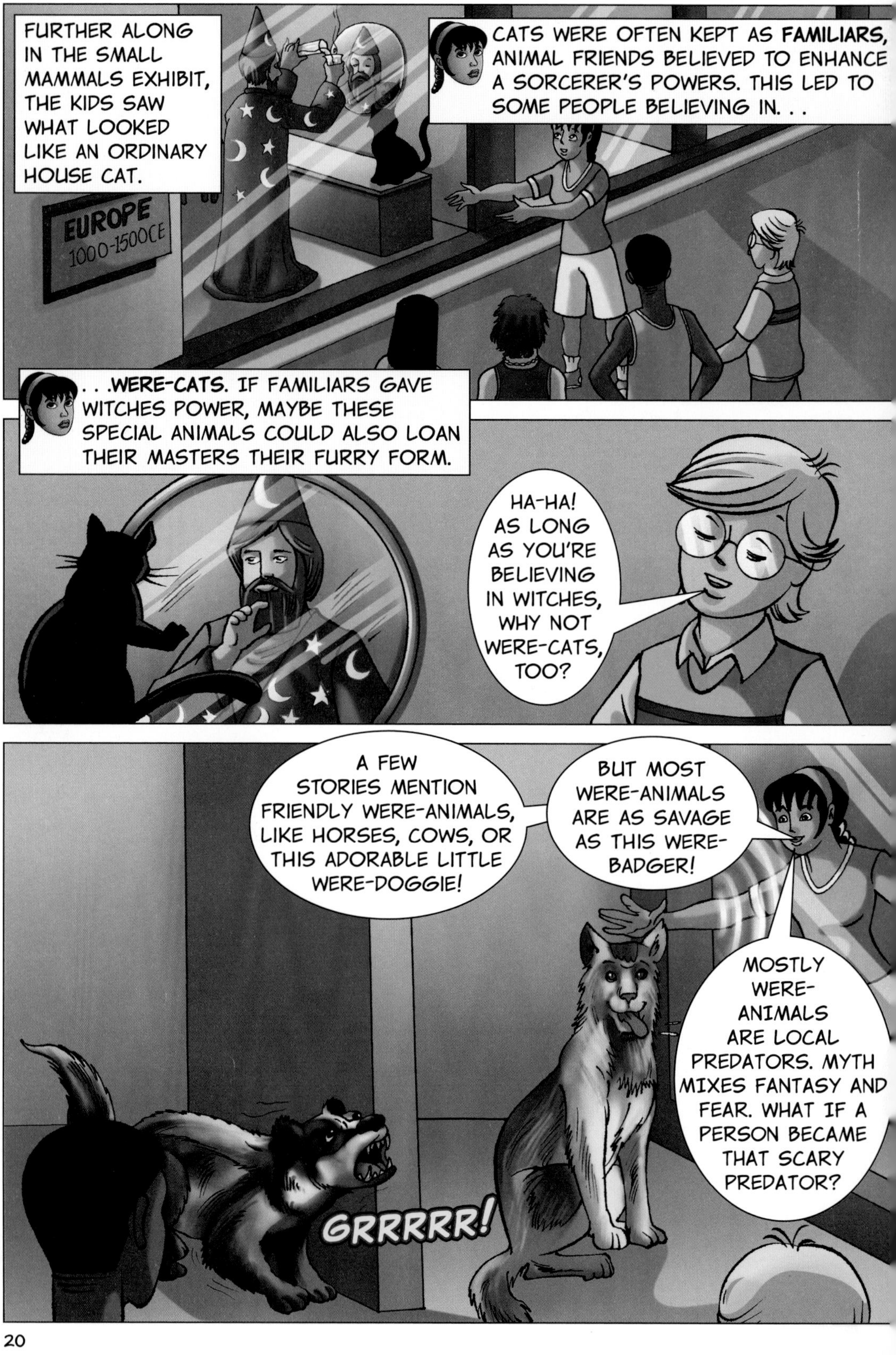
FURTHER ALONG IN THE SMALL MAMMALS EXHIBIT, THE KIDS SAW WHAT LOOKED LIKE AN ORDINARY HOUSE CAT.
CATS WERE OFTEN KEPT AS **FAMILIARS,** ANIMAL FRIENDS BELIEVED TO ENHANCE A SORCERER'S POWERS. THIS LED TO SOME PEOPLE BELIEVING IN. . .
EUROPE 1000-1500CE
. . .**WERE-CATS**. IF FAMILIARS GAVE WITCHES POWER, MAYBE THESE SPECIAL ANIMALS COULD ALSO LOAN THEIR MASTERS THEIR FURRY FORM.
HA-HA! AS LONG AS YOU'RE BELIEVING IN WITCHES, WHY NOT WERE-CATS, TOO?
A FEW STORIES MENTION FRIENDLY WERE-ANIMALS, LIKE HORSES, COWS, OR THIS ADORABLE LITTLE WERE-DOGGIE!
BUT MOST WERE-ANIMALS ARE AS SAVAGE AS THIS WERE-BADGER!
MOSTLY WERE-ANIMALS ARE LOCAL PREDATORS. MYTH MIXES FANTASY AND FEAR. WHAT IF A PERSON BECAME THAT SCARY PREDATOR?
GRRRRR!

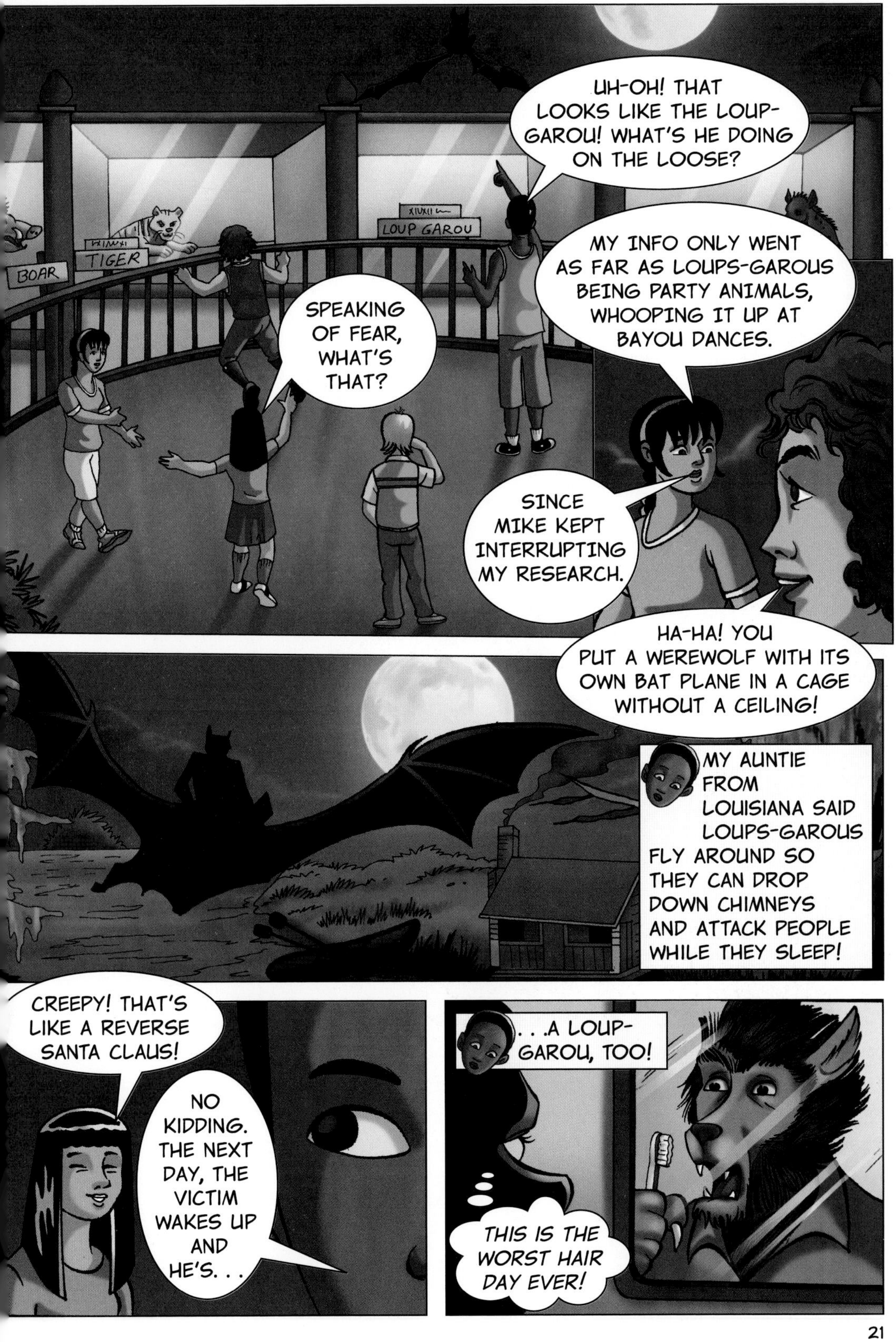
LOUP GARO U
TIGER
BOAR
UH-OH! THAT LOOKS LIKE THE LOUP-GAROU! WHAT'S HE DOING ON THE LOOSE?
SPEAKING OF FEAR, WHAT'S THAT?
MY INFO ONLY WENT AS FAR AS LOUPS-GAROUS BEING PARTY ANIMALS, WHOOPING IT UP AT BAYOU DANCES.
SINCE MIKE KEPT INTERRUPTING MY RESEARCH.
HA-HA! YOU PUT A WEREWOLF WITH ITS OWN BAT PLANE IN A CAGE WITHOUT A CEILING!
MY AUNTIE FROM LOUISIANA SAID LOUPS-GAROUS FLY AROUND SO THEY CAN DROP DOWN CHIMNEYS AND ATTACK PEOPLE WHILE THEY SLEEP!
CREEPY! THAT'S LIKE A REVERSE SANTA CLAUS!
NO KIDDING. THE NEXT DAY, THE VICTIM WAKES UP AND HE'S. . .
. . .A LOUP-GAROU, TOO!
THIS IS THE WORST HAIR DAY EVER!

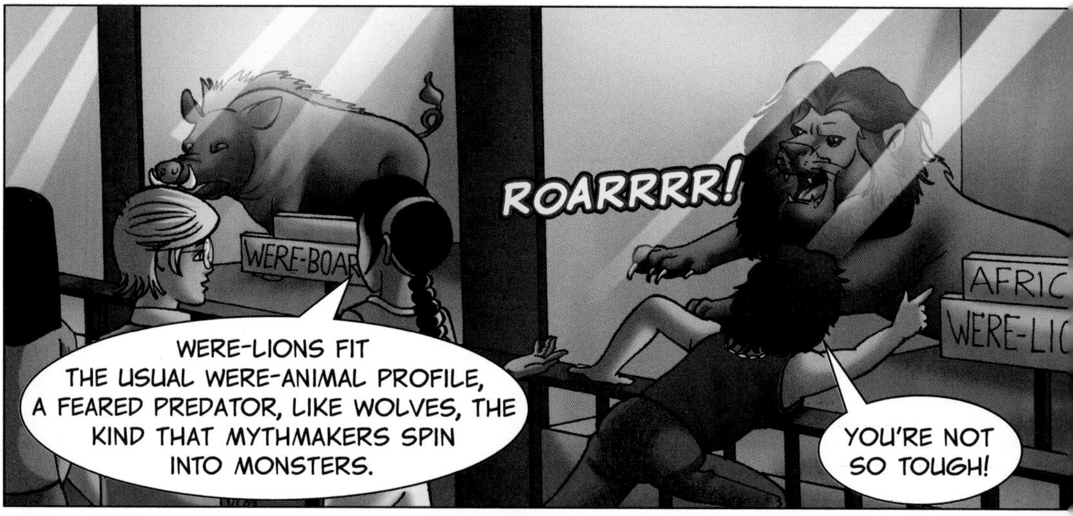
ROARRRR!
WERE-BOAR
AFRIC
WERE-LIC
WERE-LIONS FIT THE USUAL WERE-ANIMAL PROFILE, A FEARED PREDATOR, LIKE WOLVES, THE KIND THAT MYTHMAKERS SPIN INTO MONSTERS.
YOU'RE NOT SO TOUGH!

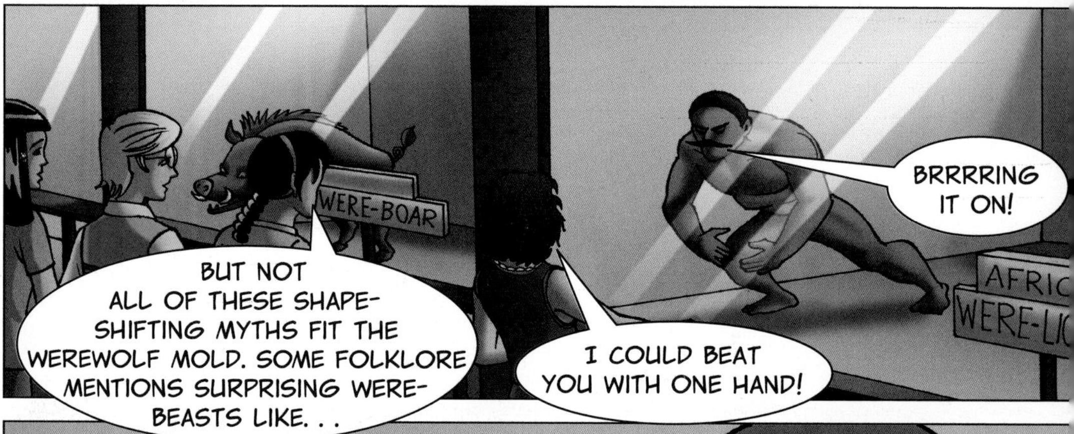
WERE-BOAR
AFRIC
WERE-LIC
BRRRRING IT ON!
BUT NOT ALL OF THESE SHAPE-SHIFTING MYTHS FIT THE WEREWOLF MOLD. SOME FOLKLORE MENTIONS SURPRISING WERE-BEASTS LIKE. . .
I COULD BEAT YOU WITH ONE HAND!

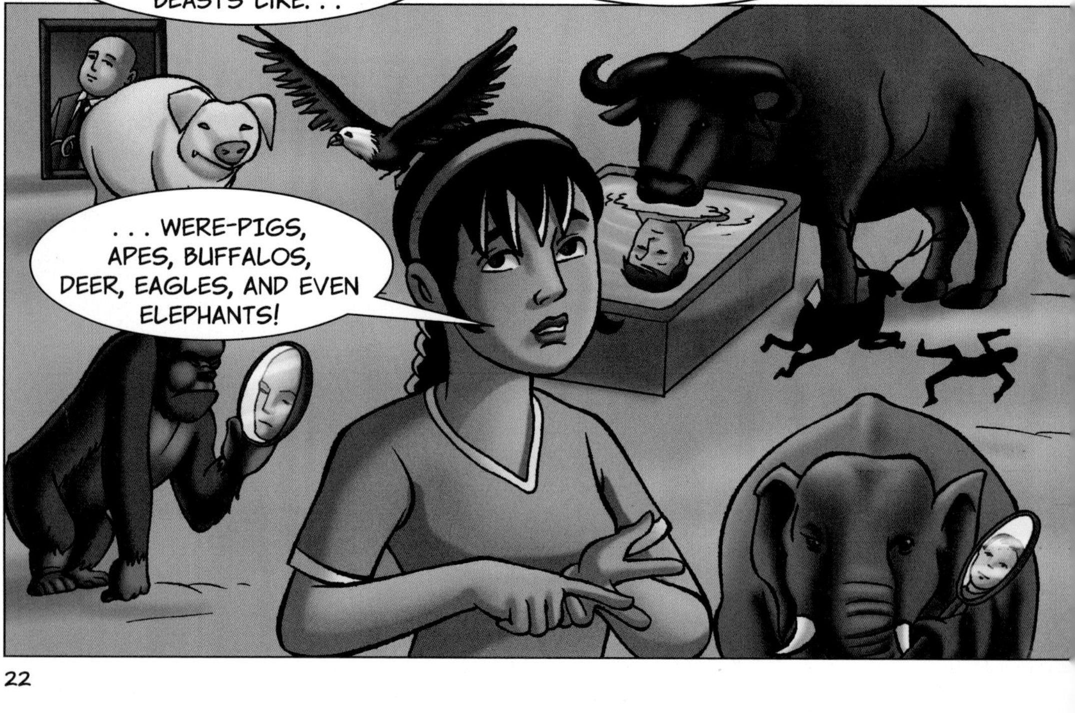
. . . WERE-PIGS, APES, BUFFALOS, DEER, EAGLES, AND EVEN ELEPHANTS!

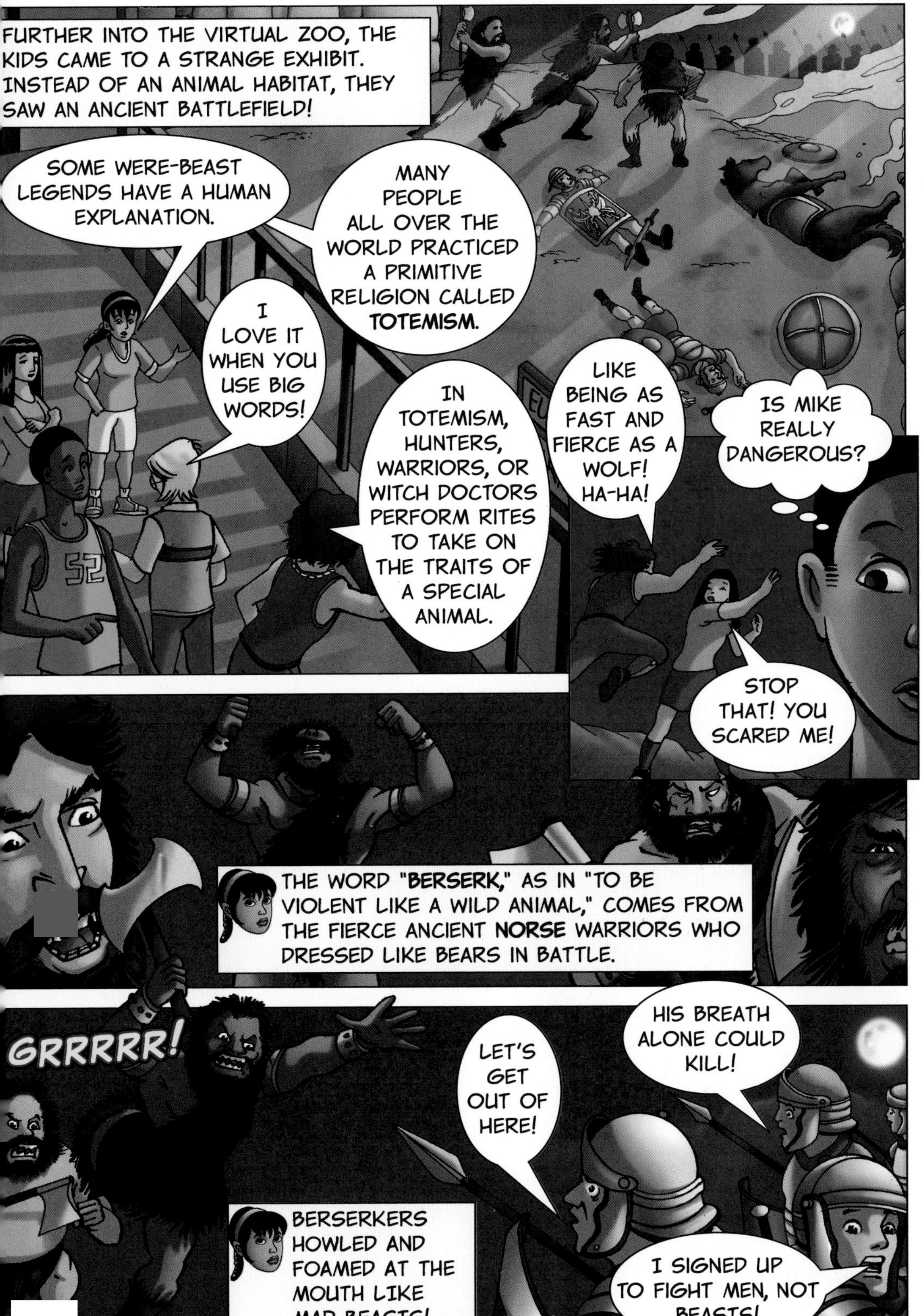
FURTHER INTO THE VIRTUAL ZOO, THE KIDS CAME TO A STRANGE EXHIBIT. INSTEAD OF AN ANIMAL HABITAT, THEY SAW AN ANCIENT BATTLEFIELD!
SOME WERE-BEAST LEGENDS HAVE A HUMAN EXPLANATION.
MANY PEOPLE ALL OVER THE WORLD PRACTICED A PRIMITIVE RELIGION CALLED **TOTEMISM.**
I LOVE IT WHEN YOU USE BIG WORDS!
IN TOTEMISM, HUNTERS, WARRIORS, OR WITCH DOCTORS PERFORM RITES TO TAKE ON THE TRAITS OF A SPECIAL ANIMAL.
LIKE BEING AS FAST AND FIERCE AS A WOLF! HA-HA!
IS MIKE REALLY DANGEROUS?
STOP THAT! YOU SCARED ME!
THE WORD "**BERSERK,**" AS IN "TO BE VIOLENT LIKE A WILD ANIMAL," COMES FROM THE FIERCE ANCIENT **NORSE** WARRIORS WHO DRESSED LIKE BEARS IN BATTLE.
GRRRRR!
LET'S GET OUT OF HERE!
HIS BREATH ALONE COULD KILL!
BERSERKERS HOWLED AND FOAMED AT THE MOUTH LIKE MAD BEASTS!
I SIGNED UP TO FIGHT MEN, NOT BEASTS!

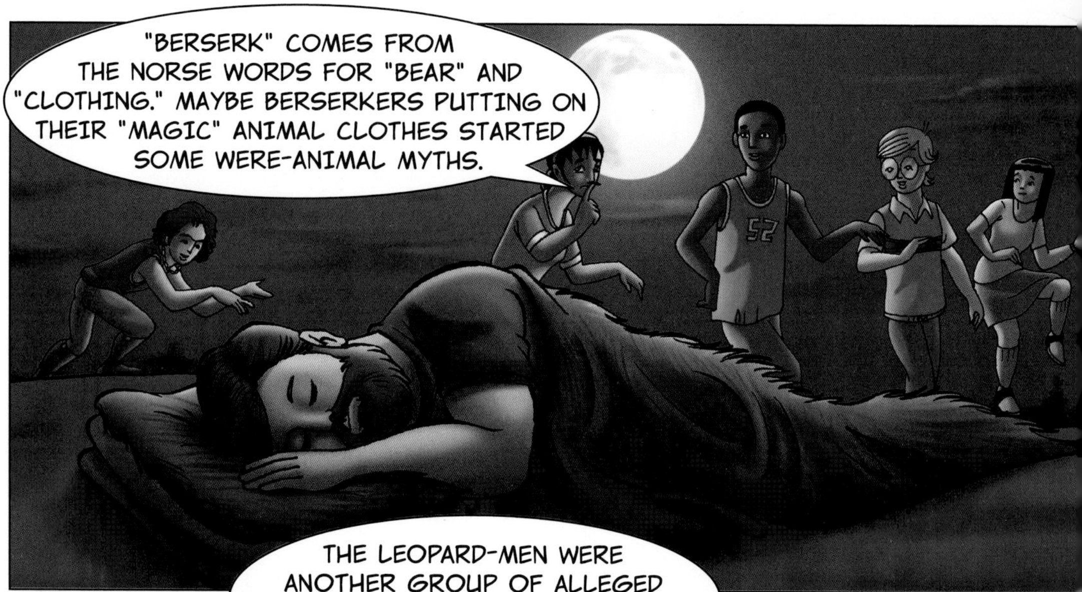
"BERSERK" COMES FROM THE NORSE WORDS FOR "BEAR" AND "CLOTHING." MAYBE BERSERKERS PUTTING ON THEIR "MAGIC" ANIMAL CLOTHES STARTED SOME WERE-ANIMAL MYTHS.
52

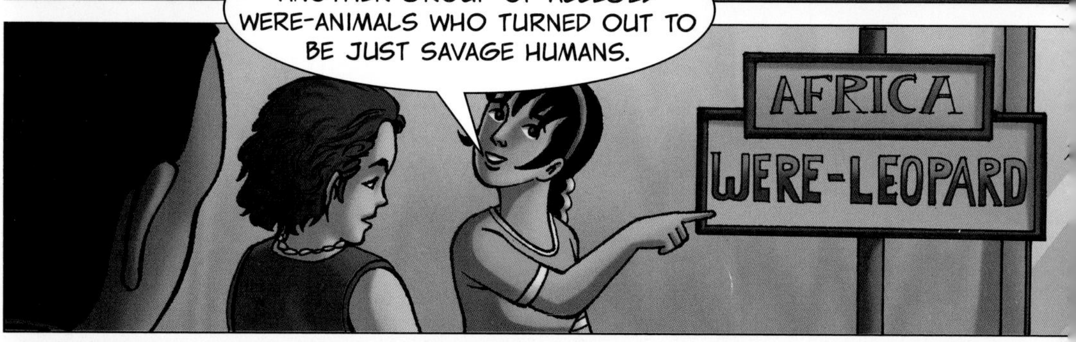
THE LEOPARD-MEN WERE ANOTHER GROUP OF ALLEGED WERE-ANIMALS WHO TURNED OUT TO BE JUST SAVAGE HUMANS.
AFRICA
WERE-LEOPARD

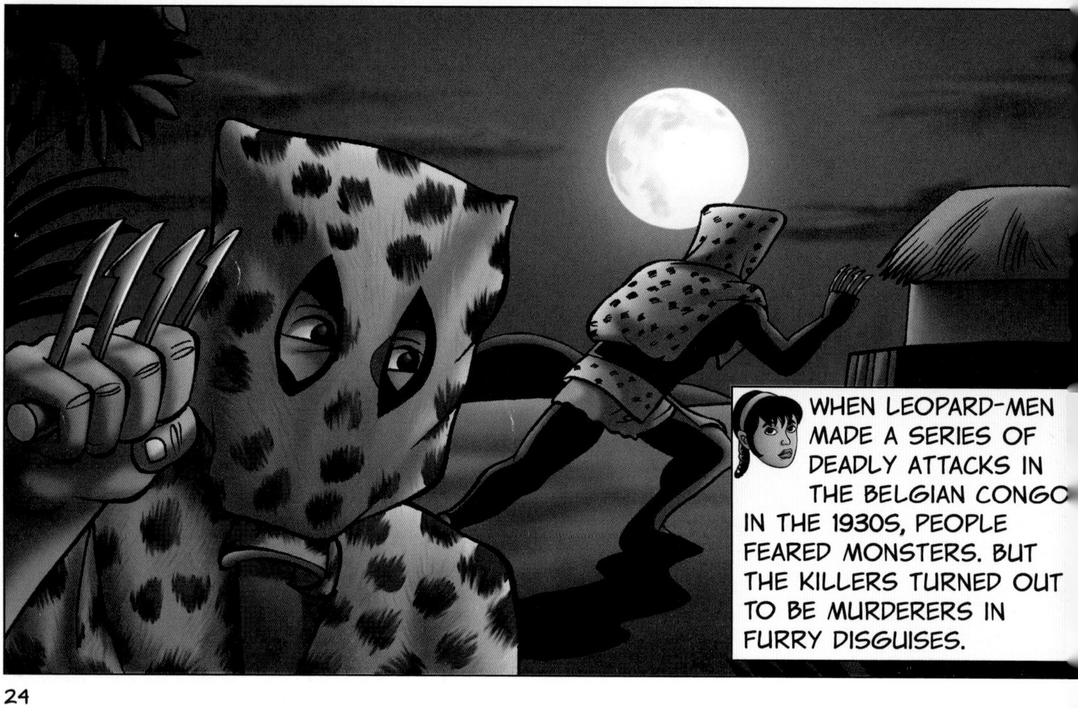
WHEN LEOPARD-MEN MADE A SERIES OF DEADLY ATTACKS IN THE BELGIAN CONGO IN THE 1930S, PEOPLE FEARED MONSTERS. BUT THE KILLERS TURNED OUT TO BE MURDERERS IN FURRY DISGUISES.

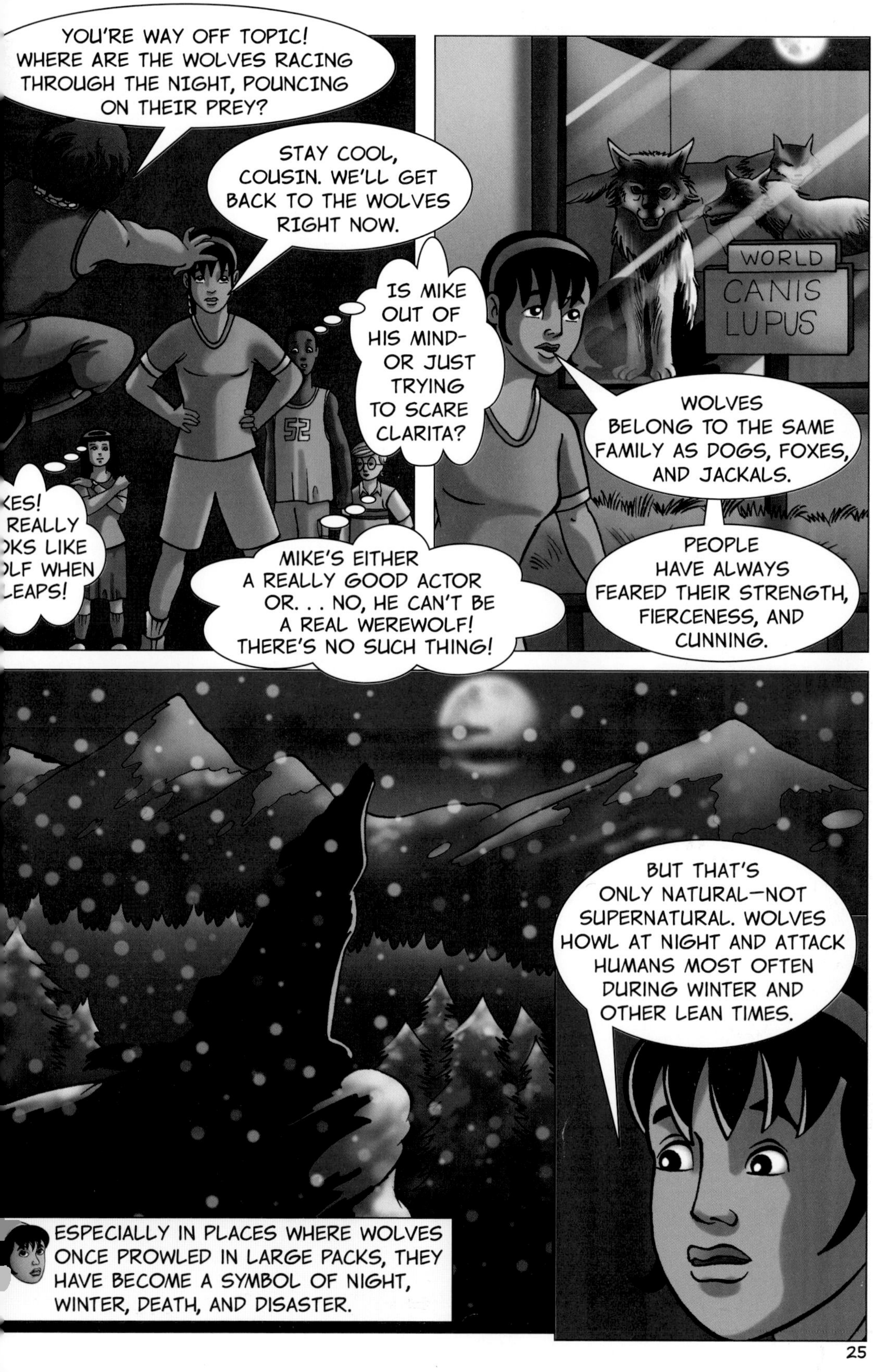

YOU'RE WAY OFF TOPIC! WHERE ARE THE WOLVES RACING THROUGH THE NIGHT, POUNCING ON THEIR PREY?
STAY COOL, COUSIN. WE'LL GET BACK TO THE WOLVES RIGHT NOW.
IS MIKE OUT OF HIS MIND- OR JUST TRYING TO SCARE CLARITA?
KES! REALLY OKS LIKE OLF WHEN LEAPS!
MIKE'S EITHER A REALLY GOOD ACTOR OR. . . NO, HE CAN'T BE A REAL WEREWOLF! THERE'S NO SUCH THING!
WORLD
CANIS LUPUS
WOLVES BELONG TO THE SAME FAMILY AS DOGS, FOXES, AND JACKALS.
PEOPLE HAVE ALWAYS FEARED THEIR STRENGTH, FIERCENESS, AND CUNNING.
BUT THAT'S ONLY NATURAL—NOT SUPERNATURAL. WOLVES HOWL AT NIGHT AND ATTACK HUMANS MOST OFTEN DURING WINTER AND OTHER LEAN TIMES.
ESPECIALLY IN PLACES WHERE WOLVES ONCE PROWLED IN LARGE PACKS, THEY HAVE BECOME A SYMBOL OF NIGHT, WINTER, DEATH, AND DISASTER.

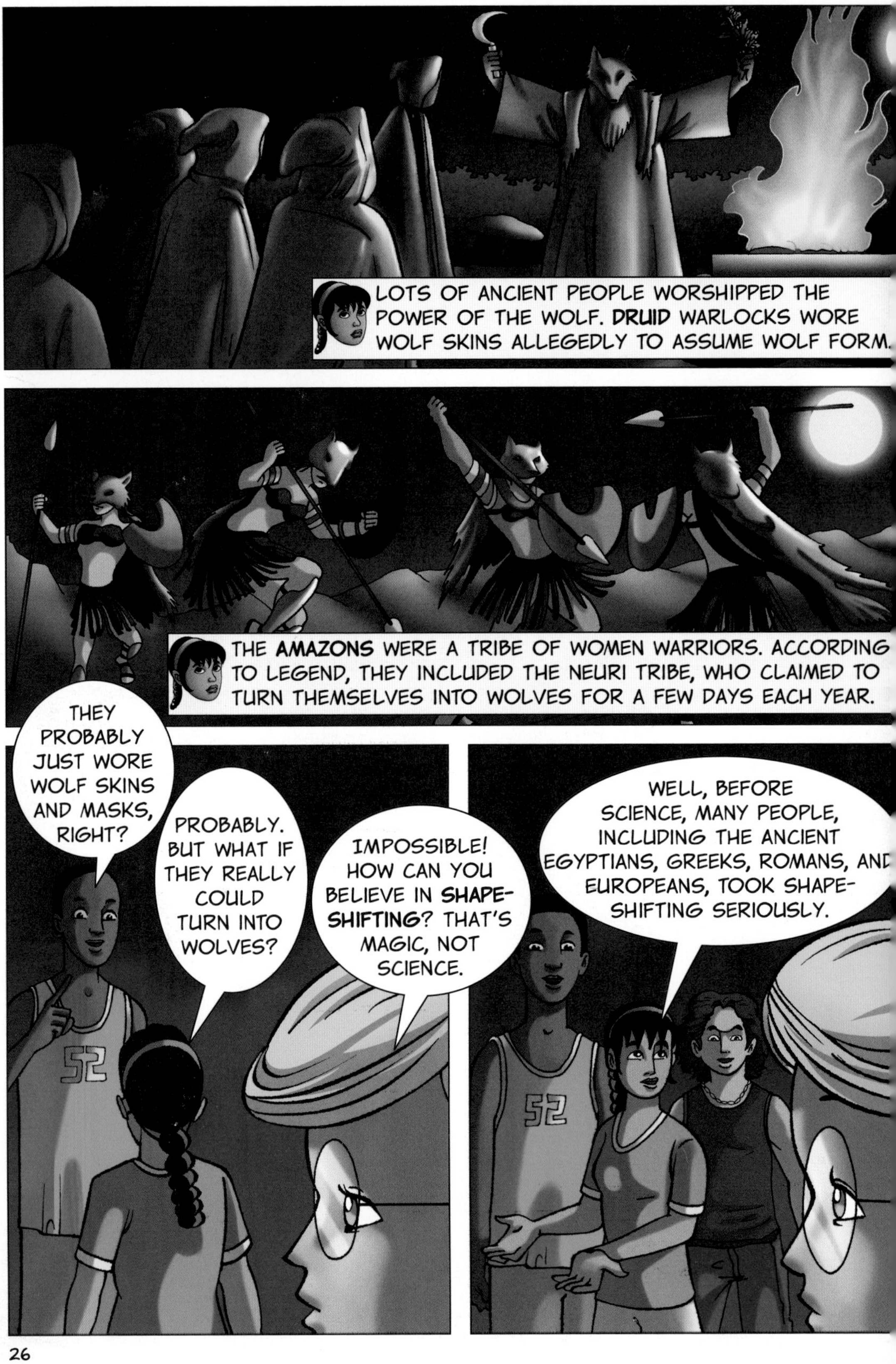
LOTS OF ANCIENT PEOPLE WORSHIPPED THE POWER OF THE WOLF. DRUID WARLOCKS WORE WOLF SKINS ALLEGEDLY TO ASSUME WOLF FORM.
THE AMAZONS WERE A TRIBE OF WOMEN WARRIORS. ACCORDING TO LEGEND, THEY INCLUDED THE NEURI TRIBE, WHO CLAIMED TO TURN THEMSELVES INTO WOLVES FOR A FEW DAYS EACH YEAR.
THEY PROBABLY JUST WORE WOLF SKINS AND MASKS, RIGHT?
PROBABLY. BUT WHAT IF THEY REALLY COULD TURN INTO WOLVES?
IMPOSSIBLE! HOW CAN YOU BELIEVE IN SHAPE-SHIFTING? THAT'S MAGIC, NOT SCIENCE.
WELL, BEFORE SCIENCE, MANY PEOPLE, INCLUDING THE ANCIENT EGYPTIANS, GREEKS, ROMANS, AND EUROPEANS, TOOK SHAPE-SHIFTING SERIOUSLY.

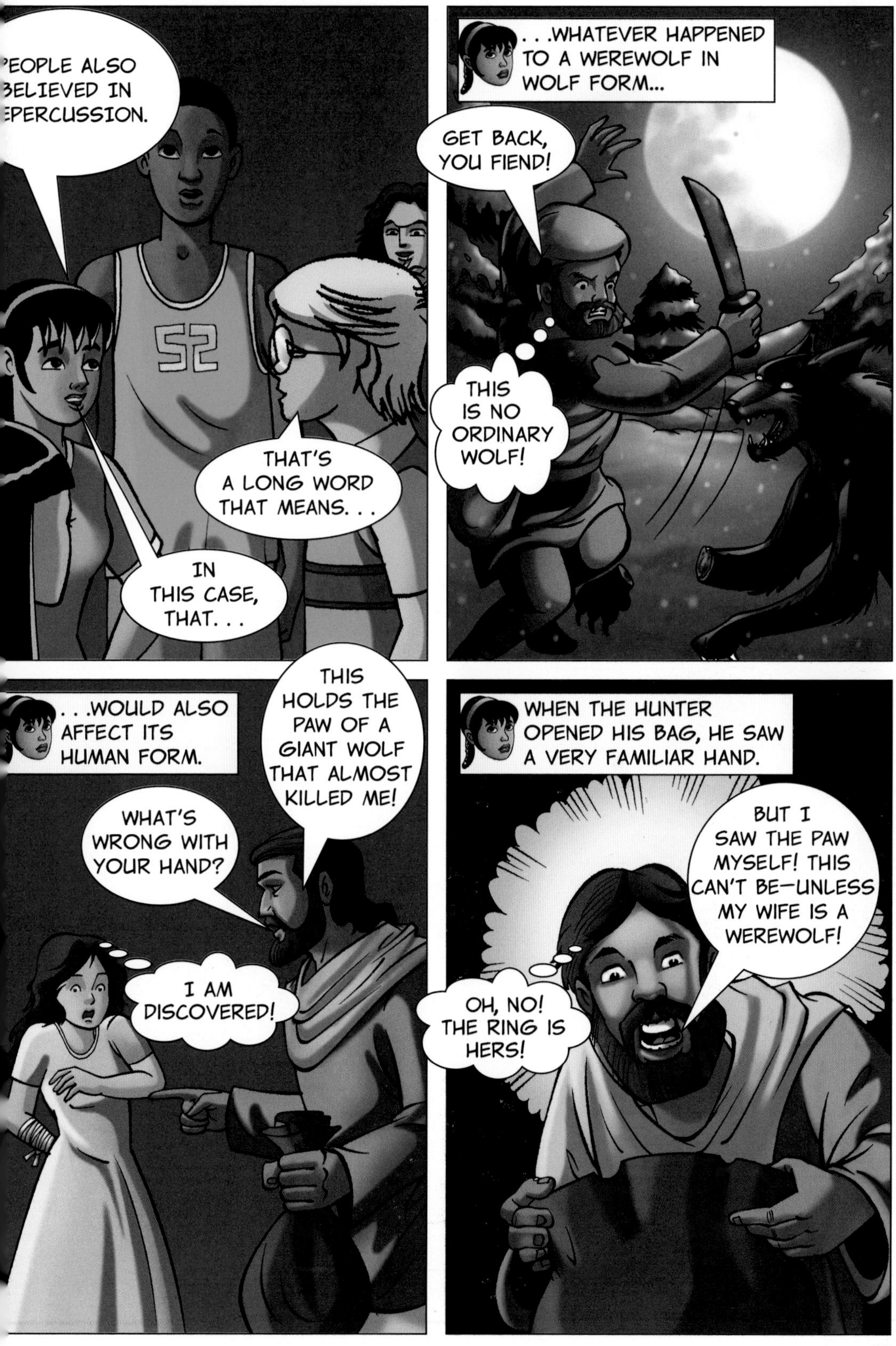
PEOPLE ALSO BELIEVED IN REPERCUSSION.
THAT'S A LONG WORD THAT MEANS. . .
IN THIS CASE, THAT. . .
. . .WHATEVER HAPPENED TO A WEREWOLF IN WOLF FORM...
GET BACK, YOU FIEND!
THIS IS NO ORDINARY WOLF!
. . .WOULD ALSO AFFECT ITS HUMAN FORM.
THIS HOLDS THE PAW OF A GIANT WOLF THAT ALMOST KILLED ME!
WHAT'S WRONG WITH YOUR HAND?
I AM DISCOVERED!
WHEN THE HUNTER OPENED HIS BAG, HE SAW A VERY FAMILIAR HAND.
BUT I SAW THE PAW MYSELF! THIS CAN'T BE—UNLESS MY WIFE IS A WEREWOLF!
OH, NO! THE RING IS HERS!

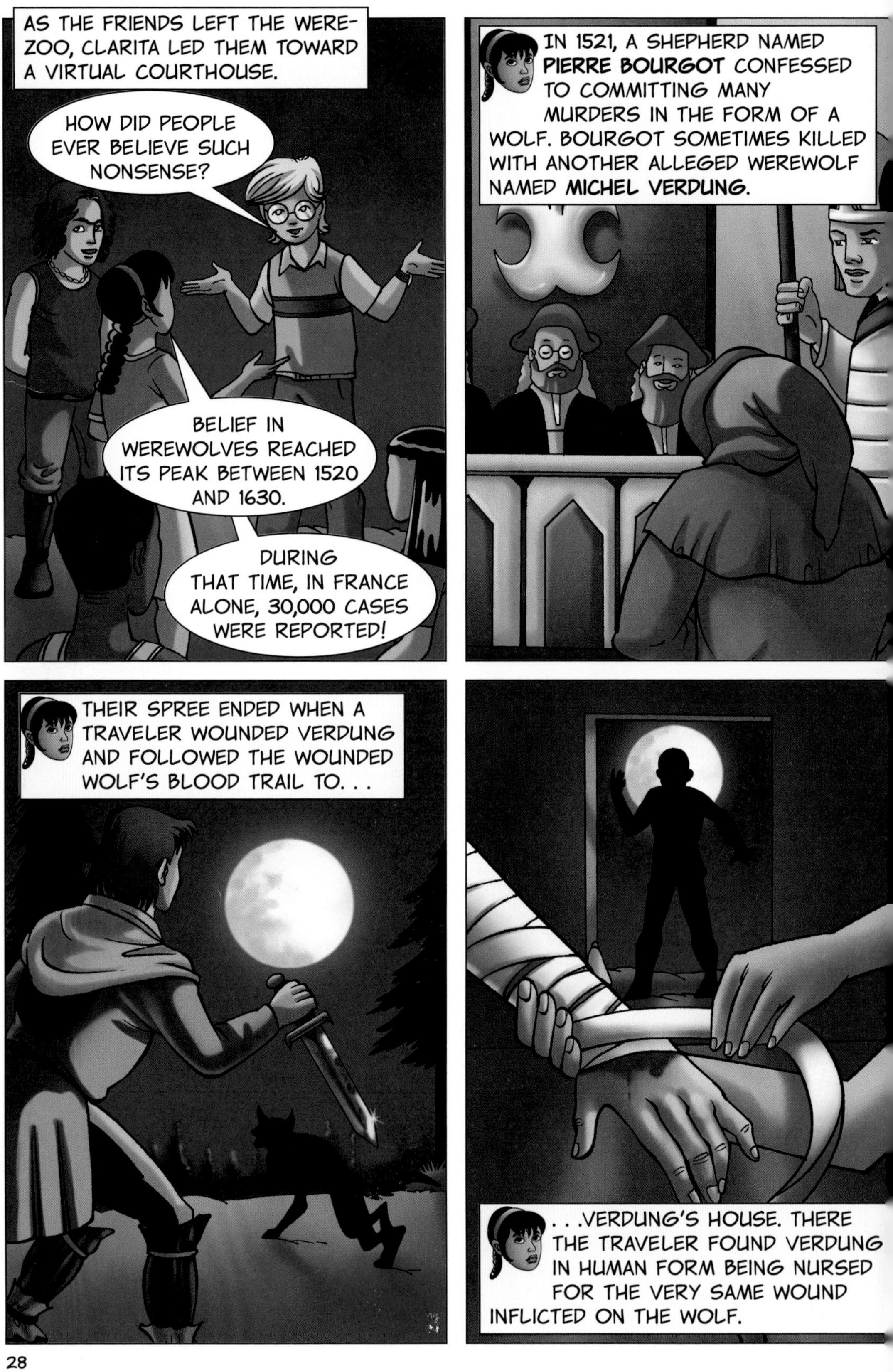
AS THE FRIENDS LEFT THE WERE-ZOO, CLARITA LED THEM TOWARD A VIRTUAL COURTHOUSE.
HOW DID PEOPLE EVER BELIEVE SUCH NONSENSE?
BELIEF IN WEREWOLVES REACHED ITS PEAK BETWEEN 1520 AND 1630.
DURING THAT TIME, IN FRANCE ALONE, 30,000 CASES WERE REPORTED!
IN 1521, A SHEPHERD NAMED **PIERRE BOURGOT** CONFESSED TO COMMITTING MANY MURDERS IN THE FORM OF A WOLF. BOURGOT SOMETIMES KILLED WITH ANOTHER ALLEGED WEREWOLF NAMED **MICHEL VERDUNG**.
THEIR SPREE ENDED WHEN A TRAVELER WOUNDED VERDUNG AND FOLLOWED THE WOUNDED WOLF'S BLOOD TRAIL TO. . .
. . .VERDUNG'S HOUSE. THERE THE TRAVELER FOUND VERDUNG IN HUMAN FORM BEING NURSED FOR THE VERY SAME WOUND INFLICTED ON THE WOLF.

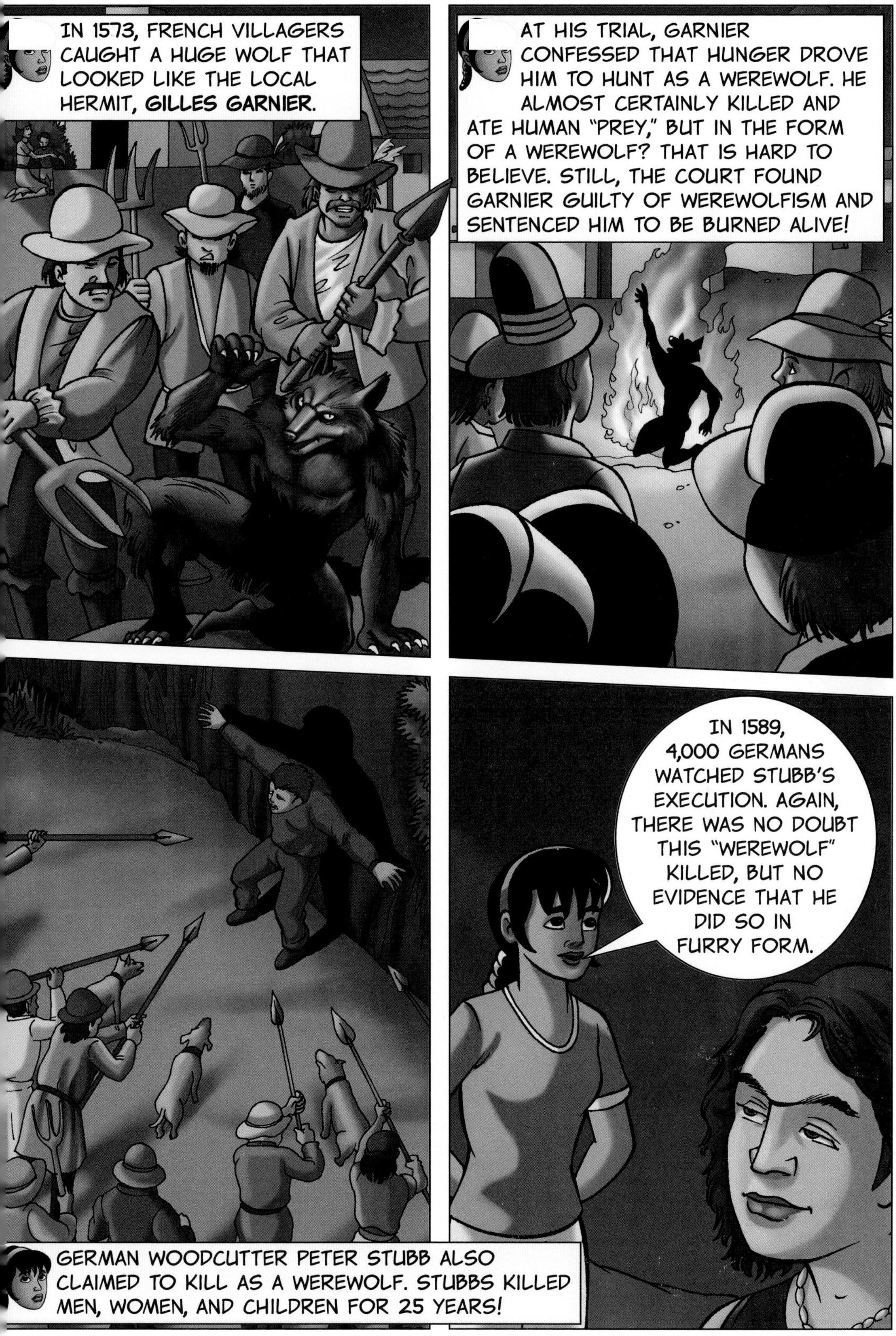
IN 1573, FRENCH VILLAGERS CAUGHT A HUGE WOLF THAT LOOKED LIKE THE LOCAL HERMIT, **GILLES GARNIER**.
AT HIS TRIAL, GARNIER CONFESSED THAT HUNGER DROVE HIM TO HUNT AS A WEREWOLF. HE ALMOST CERTAINLY KILLED AND ATE HUMAN "PREY," BUT IN THE FORM OF A WEREWOLF? THAT IS HARD TO BELIEVE. STILL, THE COURT FOUND GARNIER GUILTY OF WEREWOLFISM AND SENTENCED HIM TO BE BURNED ALIVE!
GERMAN WOODCUTTER PETER STUBB ALSO CLAIMED TO KILL AS A WEREWOLF. STUBBS KILLED MEN, WOMEN, AND CHILDREN FOR 25 YEARS!
IN 1589, 4,000 GERMANS WATCHED STUBB'S EXECUTION. AGAIN, THERE WAS NO DOUBT THIS "WEREWOLF" KILLED, BUT NO EVIDENCE THAT HE DID SO IN FURRY FORM.

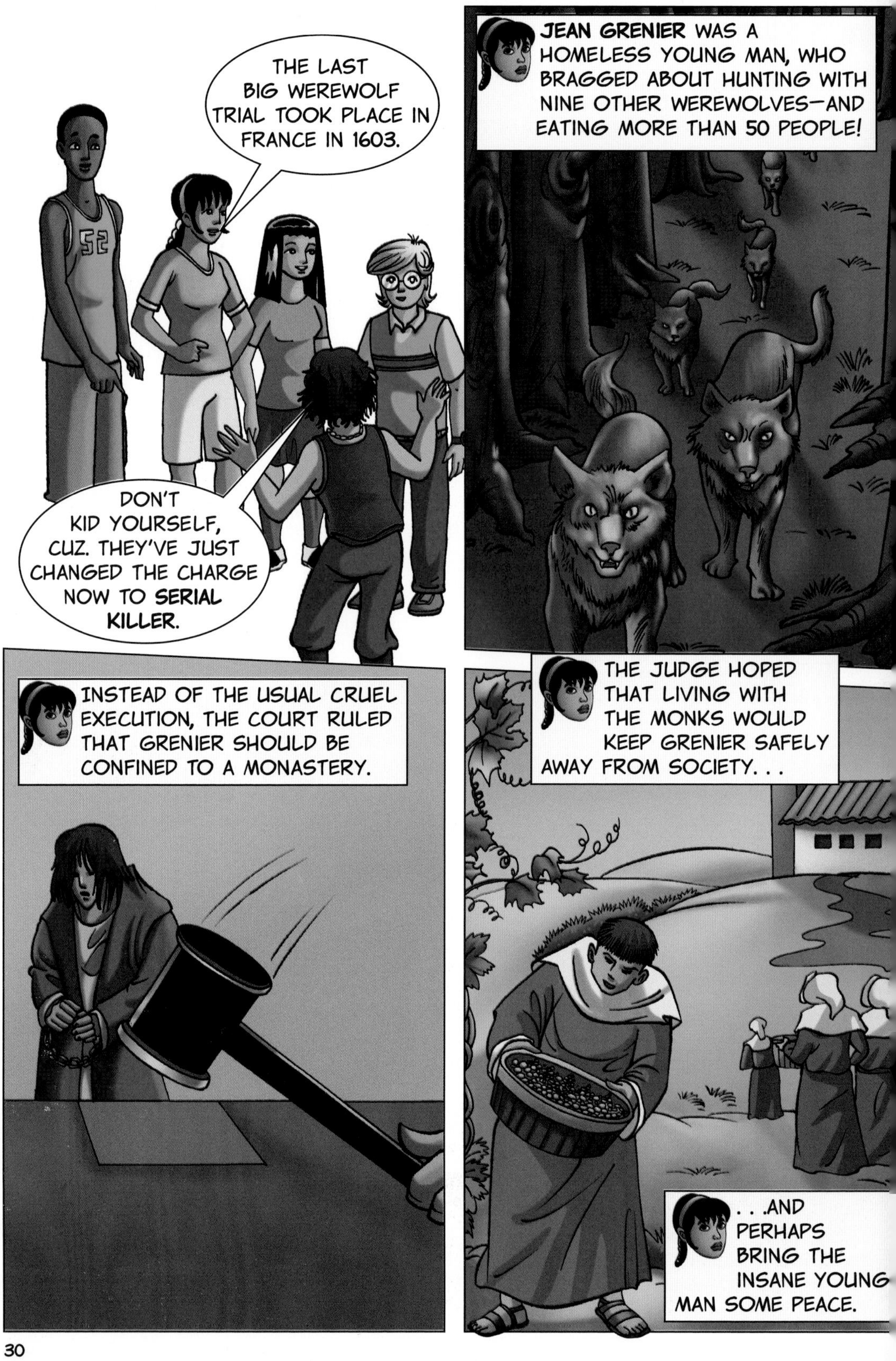
THE LAST BIG WEREWOLF TRIAL TOOK PLACE IN FRANCE IN 1603.
DON'T KID YOURSELF, CUZ. THEY'VE JUST CHANGED THE CHARGE NOW TO **SERIAL KILLER**.
JEAN GRENIER WAS A HOMELESS YOUNG MAN, WHO BRAGGED ABOUT HUNTING WITH NINE OTHER WEREWOLVES—AND EATING MORE THAN 50 PEOPLE!
INSTEAD OF THE USUAL CRUEL EXECUTION, THE COURT RULED THAT GRENIER SHOULD BE CONFINED TO A MONASTERY.
THE JUDGE HOPED THAT LIVING WITH THE MONKS WOULD KEEP GRENIER SAFELY AWAY FROM SOCIETY. . .
. . .AND PERHAPS BRING THE INSANE YOUNG MAN SOME PEACE.

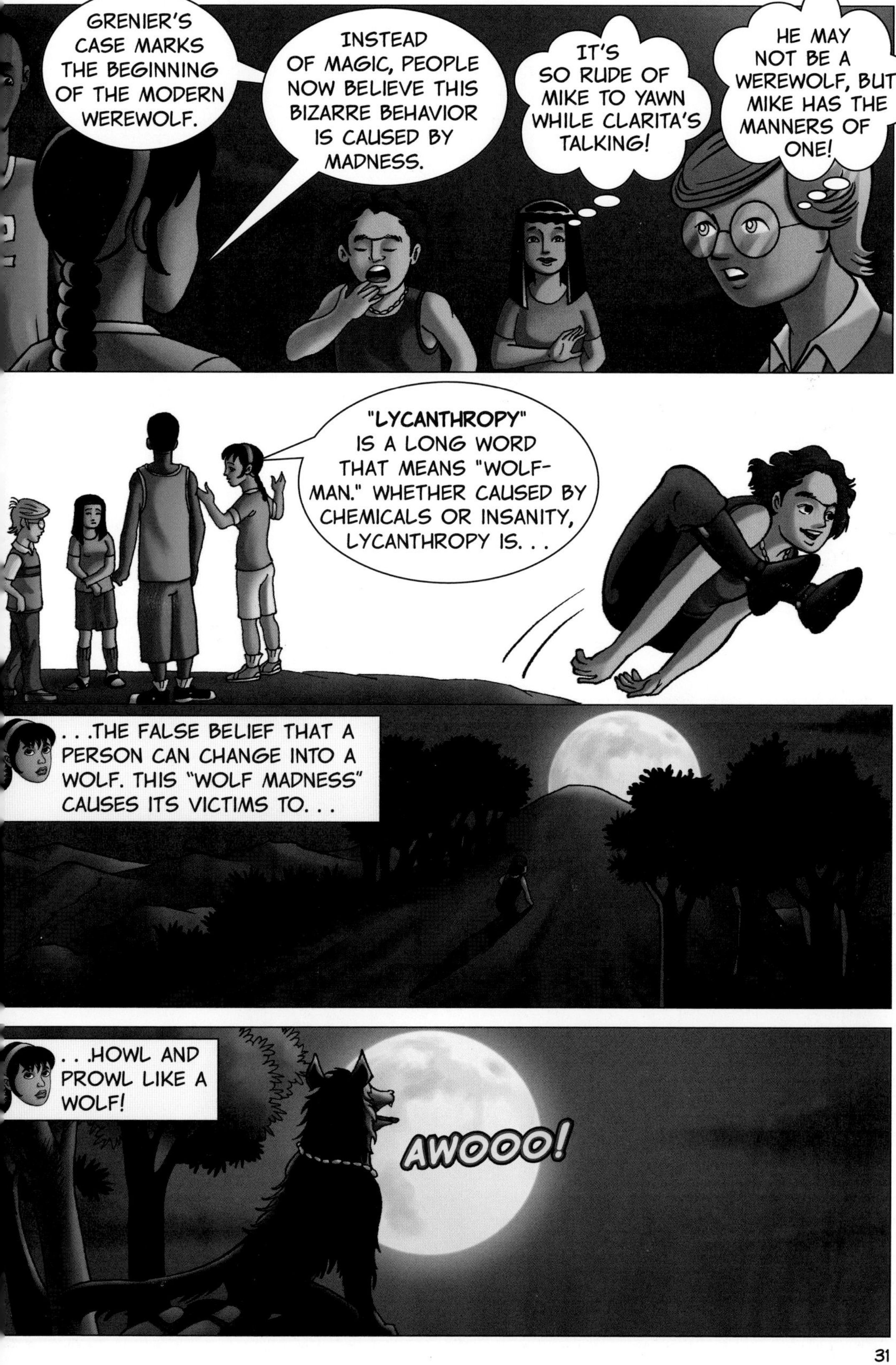
GRENIER'S CASE MARKS THE BEGINNING OF THE MODERN WEREWOLF.
INSTEAD OF MAGIC, PEOPLE NOW BELIEVE THIS BIZARRE BEHAVIOR IS CAUSED BY MADNESS.
IT'S SO RUDE OF MIKE TO YAWN WHILE CLARITA'S TALKING!
HE MAY NOT BE A WEREWOLF, BUT MIKE HAS THE MANNERS OF ONE!
"LYCANTHROPY" IS A LONG WORD THAT MEANS "WOLF-MAN." WHETHER CAUSED BY CHEMICALS OR INSANITY, LYCANTHROPY IS. . .
. . .THE FALSE BELIEF THAT A PERSON CAN CHANGE INTO A WOLF. THIS "WOLF MADNESS" CAUSES ITS VICTIMS TO. . .
. . .HOWL AND PROWL LIKE A WOLF!
AWOOO!

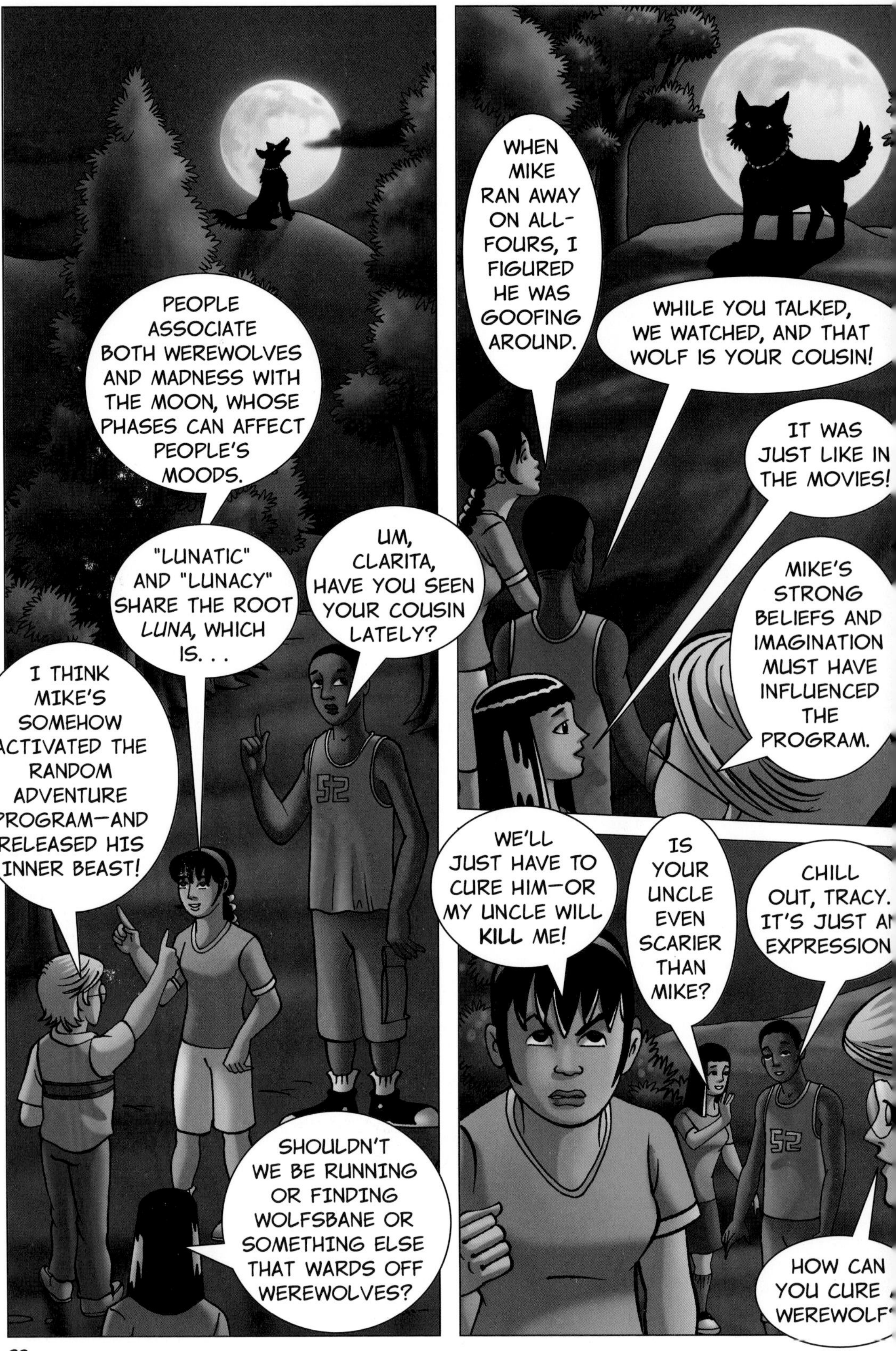

PEOPLE ASSOCIATE BOTH WEREWOLVES AND MADNESS WITH THE MOON, WHOSE PHASES CAN AFFECT PEOPLE'S MOODS.
"LUNATIC" AND "LUNACY" SHARE THE ROOT *LUNA*, WHICH IS. . .
UM, CLARITA, HAVE YOU SEEN YOUR COUSIN LATELY?
I THINK MIKE'S SOMEHOW ACTIVATED THE RANDOM ADVENTURE PROGRAM—AND RELEASED HIS INNER BEAST!
SHOULDN'T WE BE RUNNING OR FINDING WOLFSBANE OR SOMETHING ELSE THAT WARDS OFF WEREWOLVES?
WHEN MIKE RAN AWAY ON ALL-FOURS, I FIGURED HE WAS GOOFING AROUND.
WHILE YOU TALKED, WE WATCHED, AND THAT WOLF IS YOUR COUSIN!
IT WAS JUST LIKE IN THE MOVIES!
MIKE'S STRONG BELIEFS AND IMAGINATION MUST HAVE INFLUENCED THE PROGRAM.
WE'LL JUST HAVE TO CURE HIM—OR MY UNCLE WILL **KILL** ME!
IS YOUR UNCLE EVEN SCARIER THAN MIKE?
CHILL OUT, TRACY. IT'S JUST A EXPRESSION
HOW CAN YOU CURE WEREWOLF

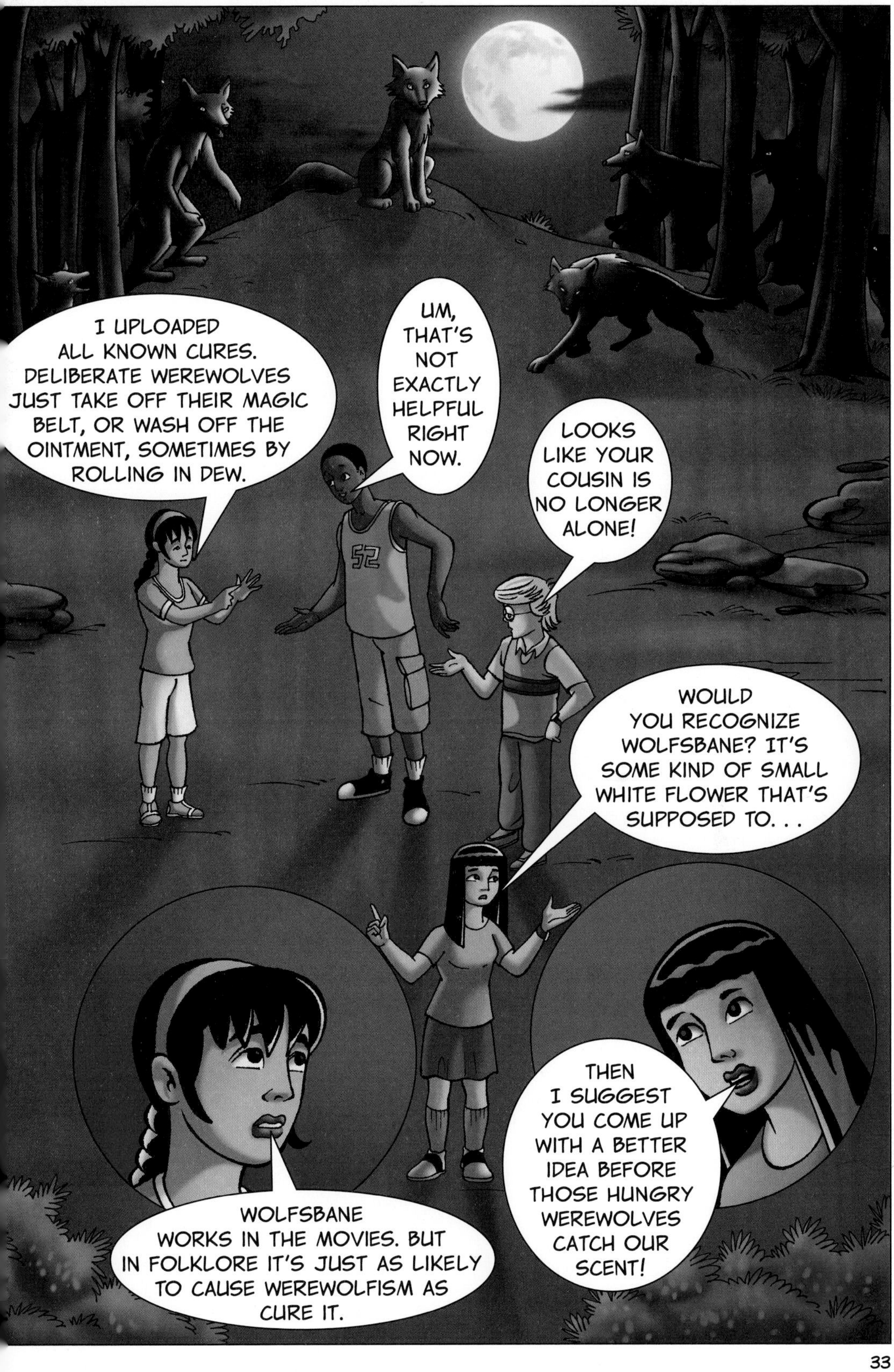
I UPLOADED ALL KNOWN CURES. DELIBERATE WEREWOLVES JUST TAKE OFF THEIR MAGIC BELT, OR WASH OFF THE OINTMENT, SOMETIMES BY ROLLING IN DEW.
UM, THAT'S NOT EXACTLY HELPFUL RIGHT NOW.
LOOKS LIKE YOUR COUSIN IS NO LONGER ALONE!
WOULD YOU RECOGNIZE WOLFSBANE? IT'S SOME KIND OF SMALL WHITE FLOWER THAT'S SUPPOSED TO. . .
WOLFSBANE WORKS IN THE MOVIES. BUT IN FOLKLORE IT'S JUST AS LIKELY TO CAUSE WEREWOLFISM AS CURE IT.
THEN I SUGGEST YOU COME UP WITH A BETTER IDEA BEFORE THOSE HUNGRY WEREWOLVES CATCH OUR SCENT!

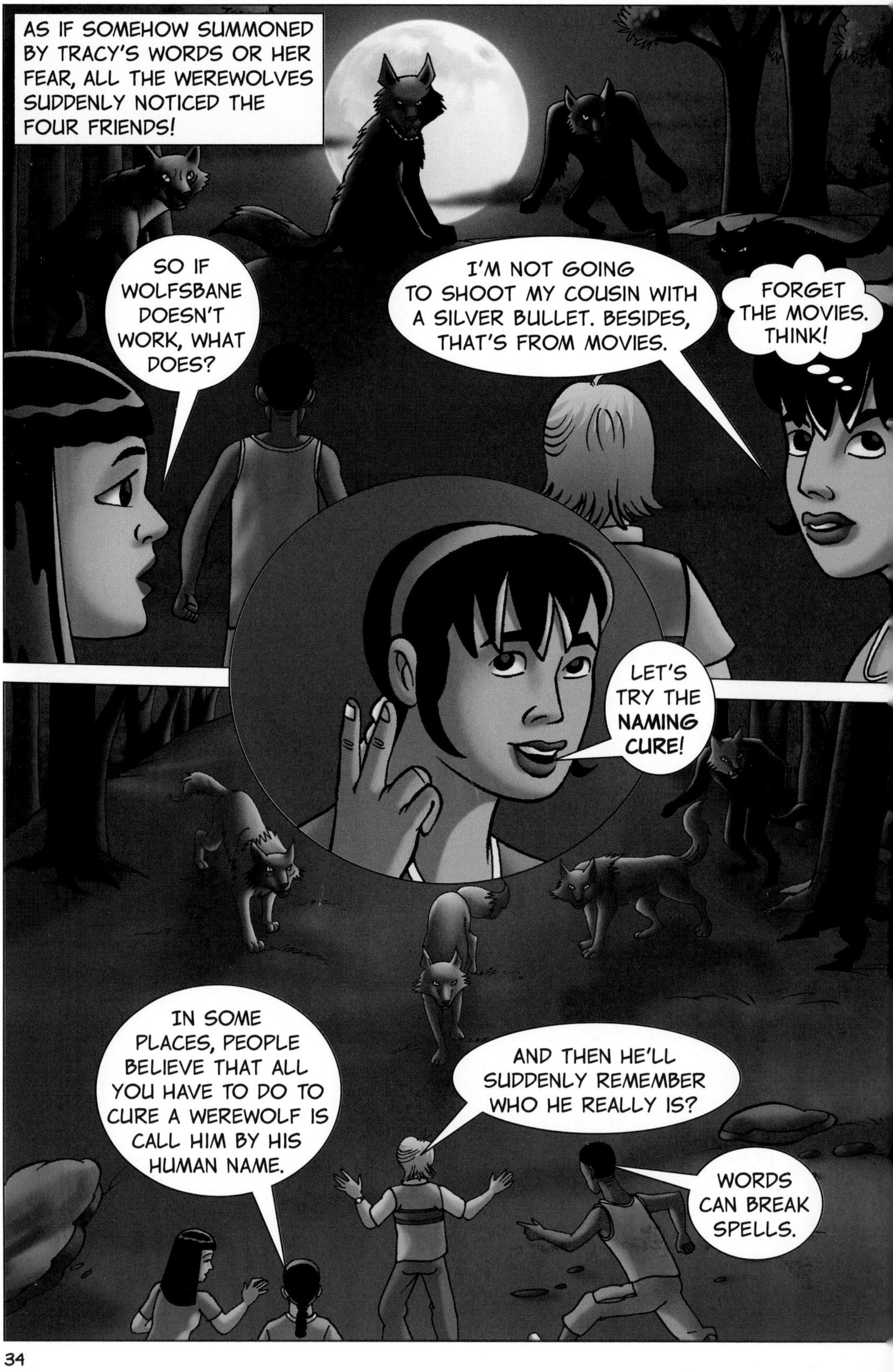
AS IF SOMEHOW SUMMONED BY TRACY'S WORDS OR HER FEAR, ALL THE WEREWOLVES SUDDENLY NOTICED THE FOUR FRIENDS!
SO IF WOLFSBANE DOESN'T WORK, WHAT DOES?
I'M NOT GOING TO SHOOT MY COUSIN WITH A SILVER BULLET. BESIDES, THAT'S FROM MOVIES.
FORGET THE MOVIES. THINK!
LET'S TRY THE **NAMING CURE!**
IN SOME PLACES, PEOPLE BELIEVE THAT ALL YOU HAVE TO DO TO CURE A WEREWOLF IS CALL HIM BY HIS HUMAN NAME.
AND THEN HE'LL SUDDENLY REMEMBER WHO HE REALLY IS?
WORDS CAN BREAK SPELLS.

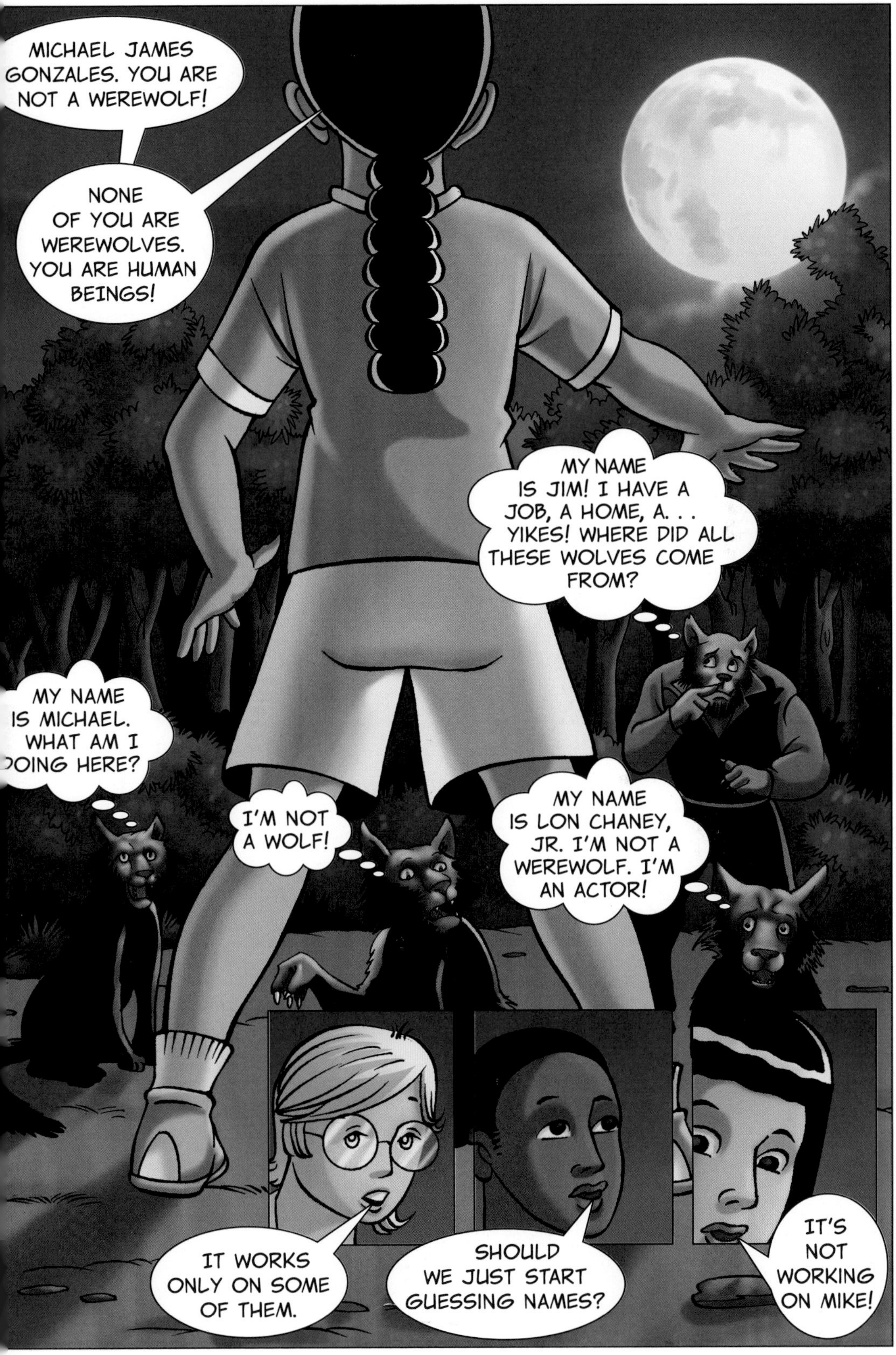
MICHAEL JAMES GONZALES. YOU ARE NOT A WEREWOLF!
NONE OF YOU ARE WEREWOLVES. YOU ARE HUMAN BEINGS!
MY NAME IS JIM! I HAVE A JOB, A HOME, A. . . YIKES! WHERE DID ALL THESE WOLVES COME FROM?
MY NAME IS MICHAEL. WHAT AM I DOING HERE?
I'M NOT A WOLF!
MY NAME IS LON CHANEY, JR. I'M NOT A WEREWOLF. I'M AN ACTOR!
IT WORKS ONLY ON SOME OF THEM.
SHOULD WE JUST START GUESSING NAMES?
IT'S NOT WORKING ON MIKE!

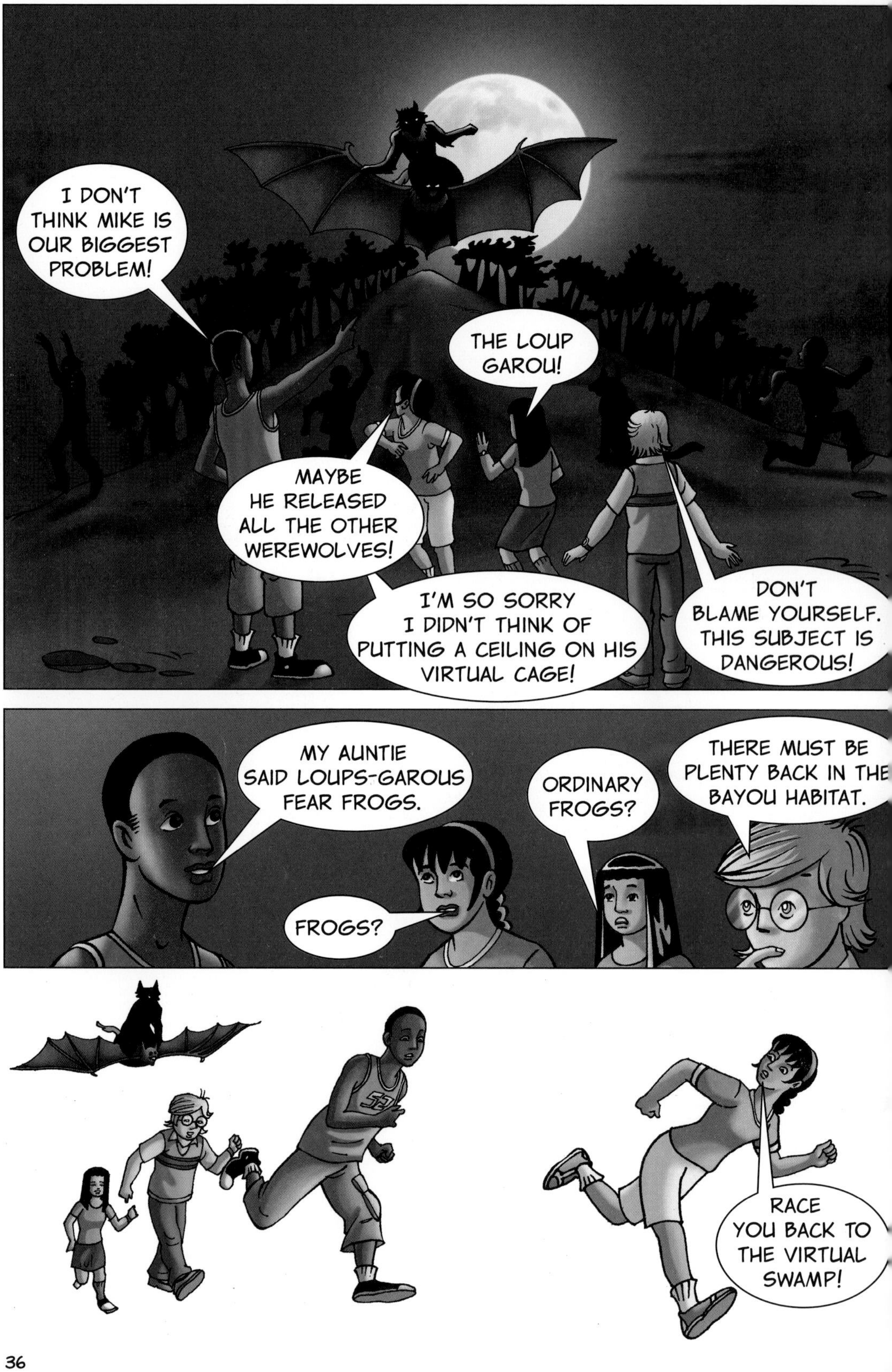
I DON'T THINK MIKE IS OUR BIGGEST PROBLEM!
THE LOUP GAROU!
MAYBE HE RELEASED ALL THE OTHER WEREWOLVES!
I'M SO SORRY I DIDN'T THINK OF PUTTING A CEILING ON HIS VIRTUAL CAGE!
DON'T BLAME YOURSELF. THIS SUBJECT IS DANGEROUS!
MY AUNTIE SAID LOUPS-GAROUS FEAR FROGS.
FROGS?
ORDINARY FROGS?
THERE MUST BE PLENTY BACK IN THE BAYOU HABITAT.
RACE YOU BACK TO THE VIRTUAL SWAMP!

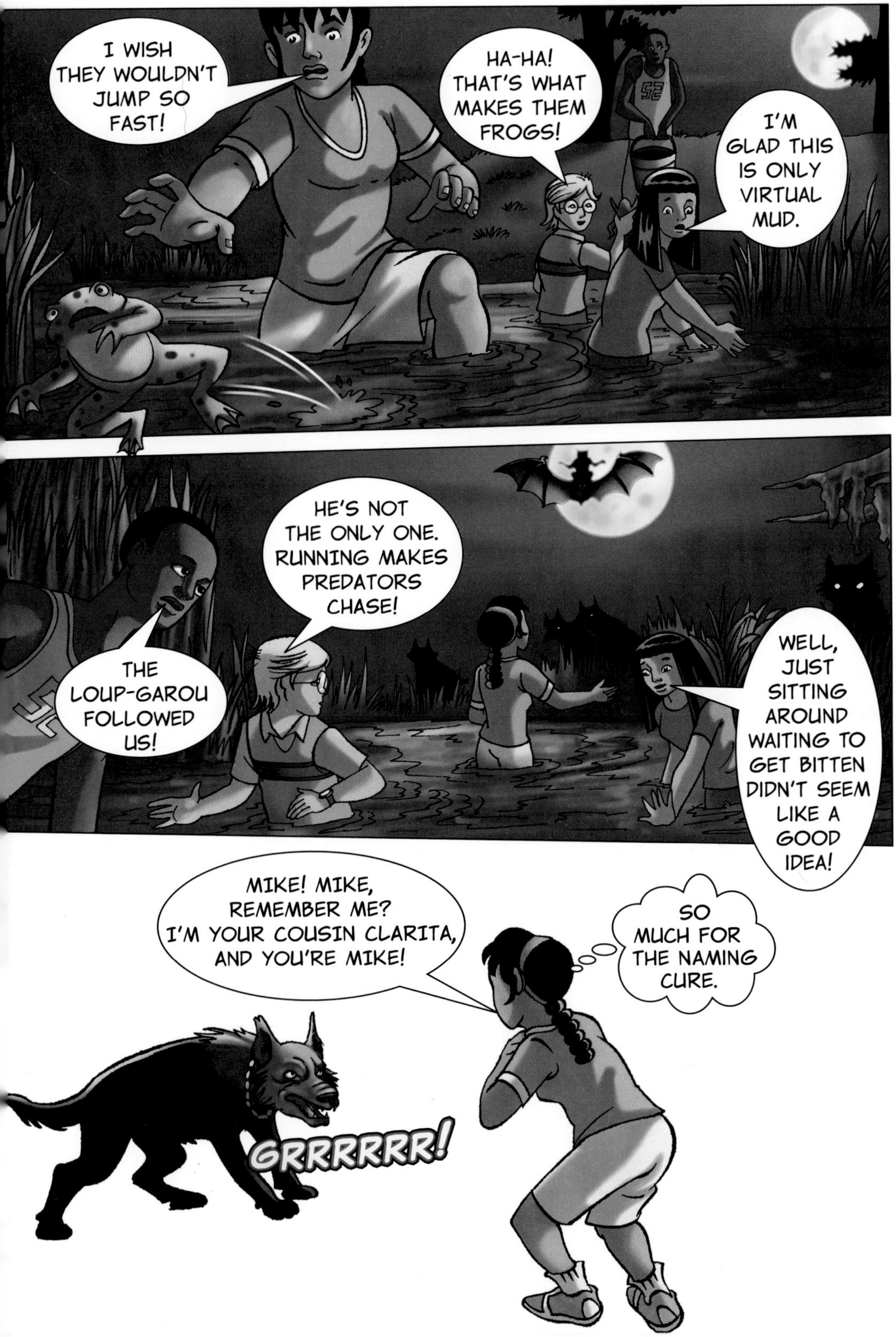
I WISH THEY WOULDN'T JUMP SO FAST!
HA-HA! THAT'S WHAT MAKES THEM FROGS!
I'M GLAD THIS IS ONLY VIRTUAL MUD.
THE LOUP-GAROU FOLLOWED US!
HE'S NOT THE ONLY ONE. RUNNING MAKES PREDATORS CHASE!
WELL, JUST SITTING AROUND WAITING TO GET BITTEN DIDN'T SEEM LIKE A GOOD IDEA!
MIKE! MIKE, REMEMBER ME? I'M YOUR COUSIN CLARITA, AND YOU'RE MIKE!
SO MUCH FOR THE NAMING CURE.
GRRRRRR!

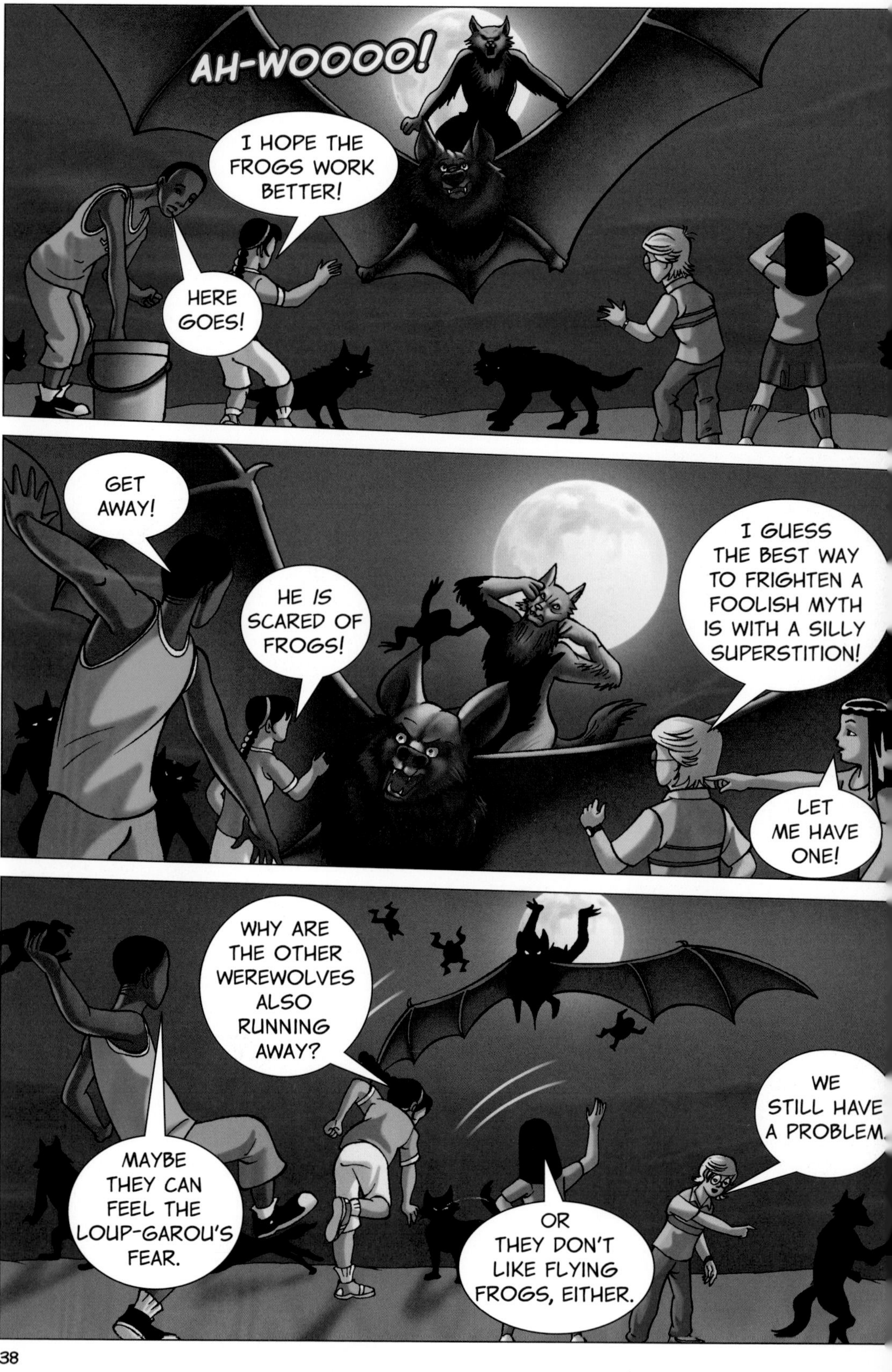
AH-WOOOO!
I HOPE THE FROGS WORK BETTER!
HERE GOES!
GET AWAY!
HE IS SCARED OF FROGS!
I GUESS THE BEST WAY TO FRIGHTEN A FOOLISH MYTH IS WITH A SILLY SUPERSTITION!
LET ME HAVE ONE!
WHY ARE THE OTHER WEREWOLVES ALSO RUNNING AWAY?
MAYBE THEY CAN FEEL THE LOUP-GAROU'S FEAR.
OR THEY DON'T LIKE FLYING FROGS, EITHER.
WE STILL HAVE A PROBLEM.

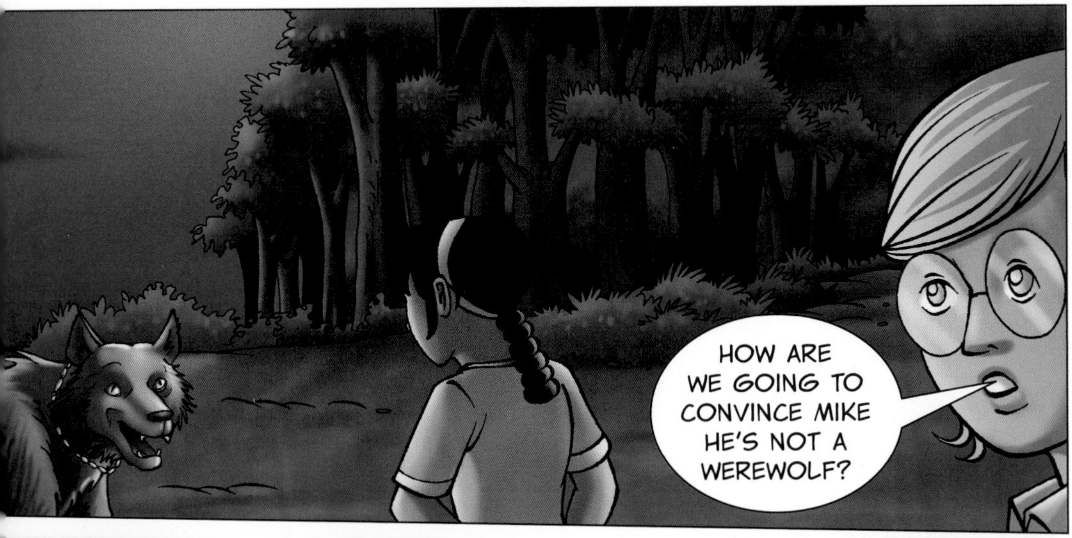
HOW ARE WE GOING TO CONVINCE MIKE HE'S NOT A WEREWOLF?

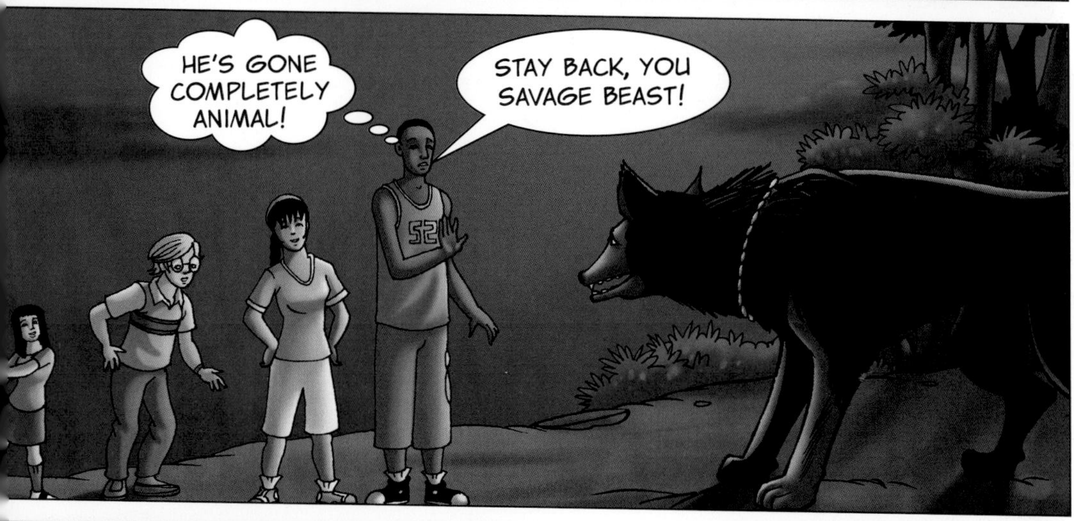
HE'S GONE COMPLETELY ANIMAL!
STAY BACK, YOU SAVAGE BEAST!

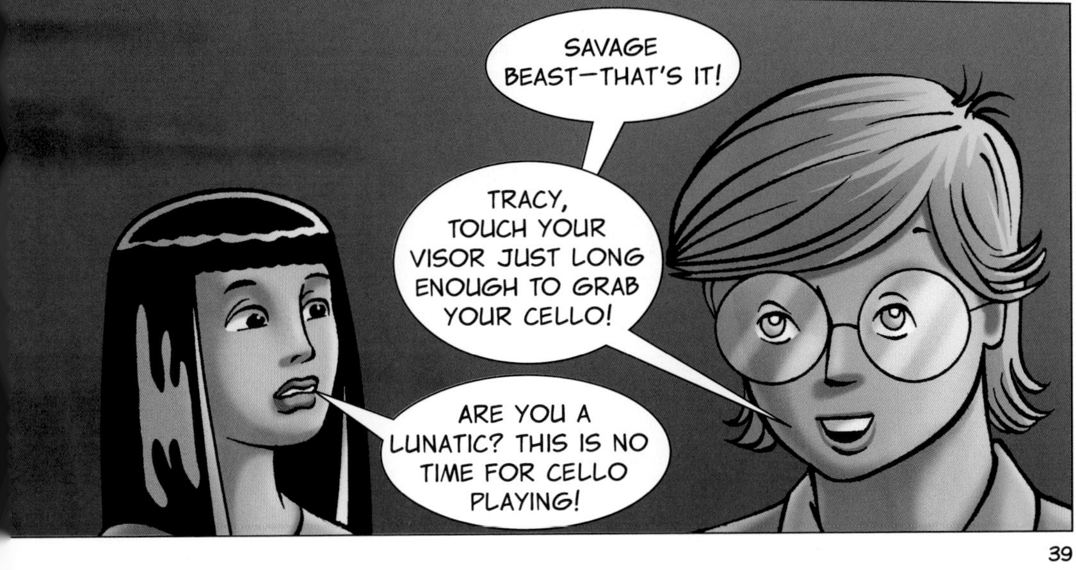
SAVAGE BEAST—THAT'S IT!
TRACY, TOUCH YOUR VISOR JUST LONG ENOUGH TO GRAB YOUR CELLO!
ARE YOU A LUNATIC? THIS IS NO TIME FOR CELLO PLAYING!

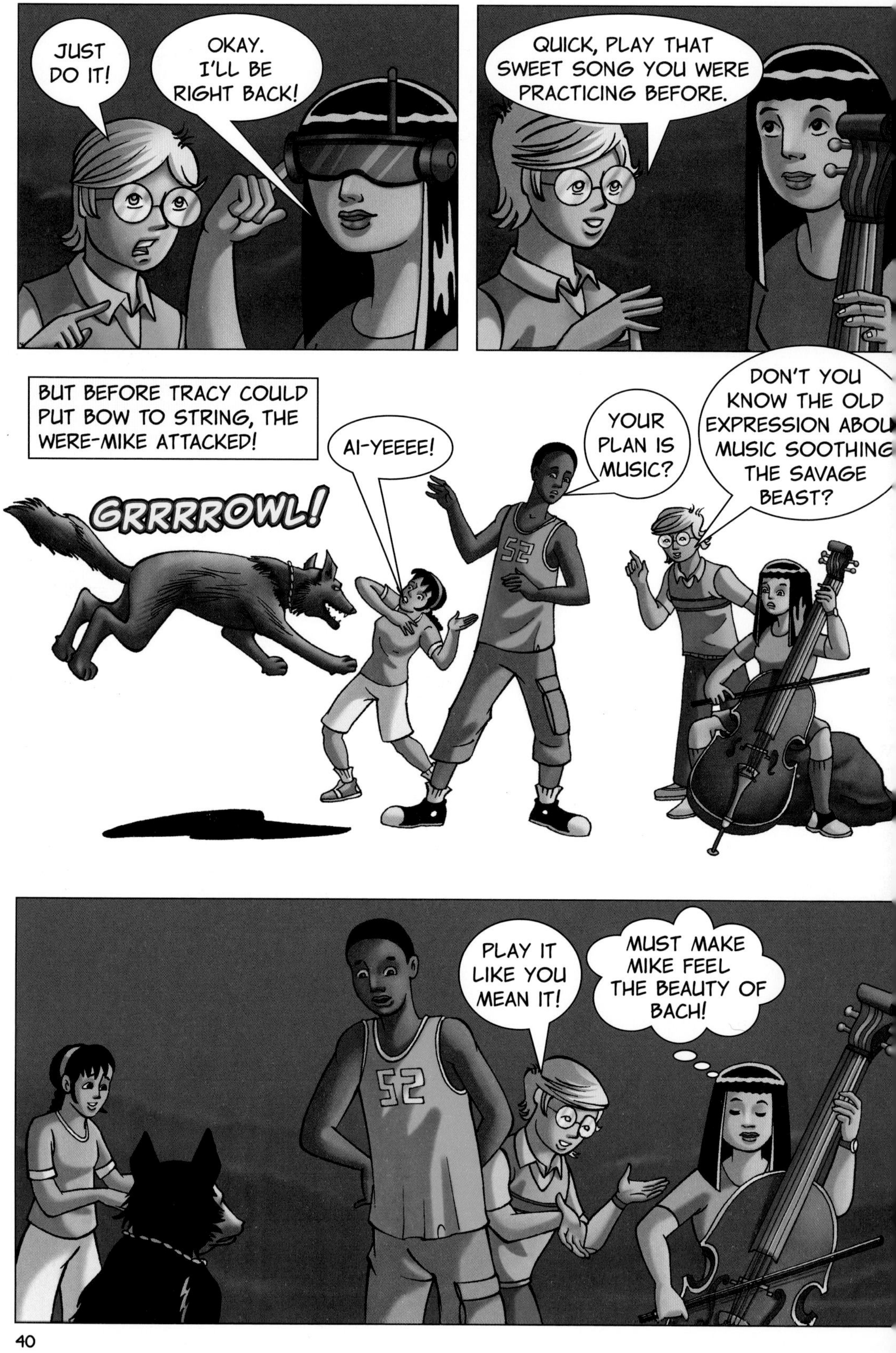
JUST DO IT!
OKAY. I'LL BE RIGHT BACK!
QUICK, PLAY THAT SWEET SONG YOU WERE PRACTICING BEFORE.
BUT BEFORE TRACY COULD PUT BOW TO STRING, THE WERE-MIKE ATTACKED!
GRRRROWL!
AI-YEEEE!
YOUR PLAN IS MUSIC?
DON'T YOU KNOW THE OLD EXPRESSION ABOU MUSIC SOOTHING THE SAVAGE BEAST?
PLAY IT LIKE YOU MEAN IT!
MUST MAKE MIKE FEEL THE BEAUTY OF BACH!

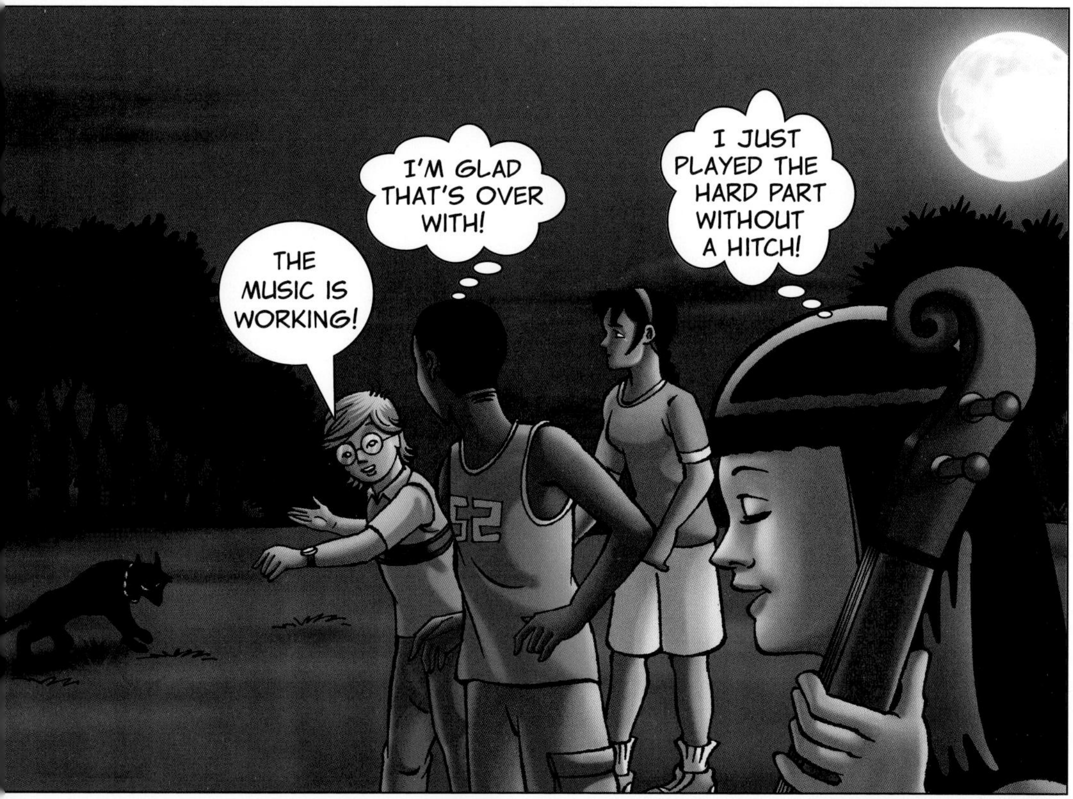
THE MUSIC IS WORKING!
I'M GLAD THAT'S OVER WITH!
I JUST PLAYED THE HARD PART WITHOUT A HITCH!

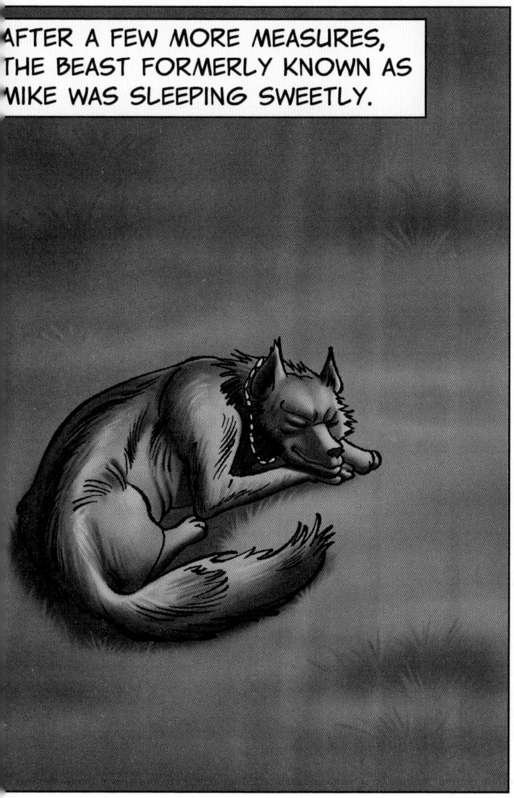
AFTER A FEW MORE MEASURES, THE BEAST FORMERLY KNOWN AS MIKE WAS SLEEPING SWEETLY.

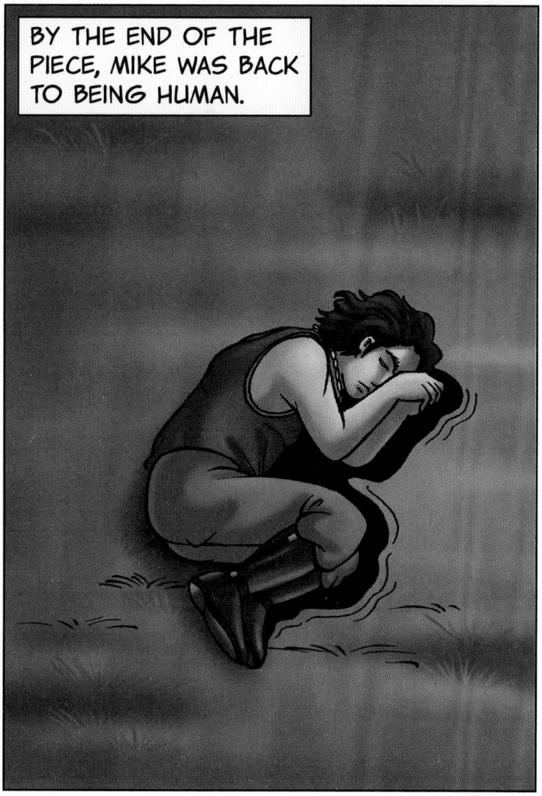
BY THE END OF THE PIECE, MIKE WAS BACK TO BEING HUMAN.

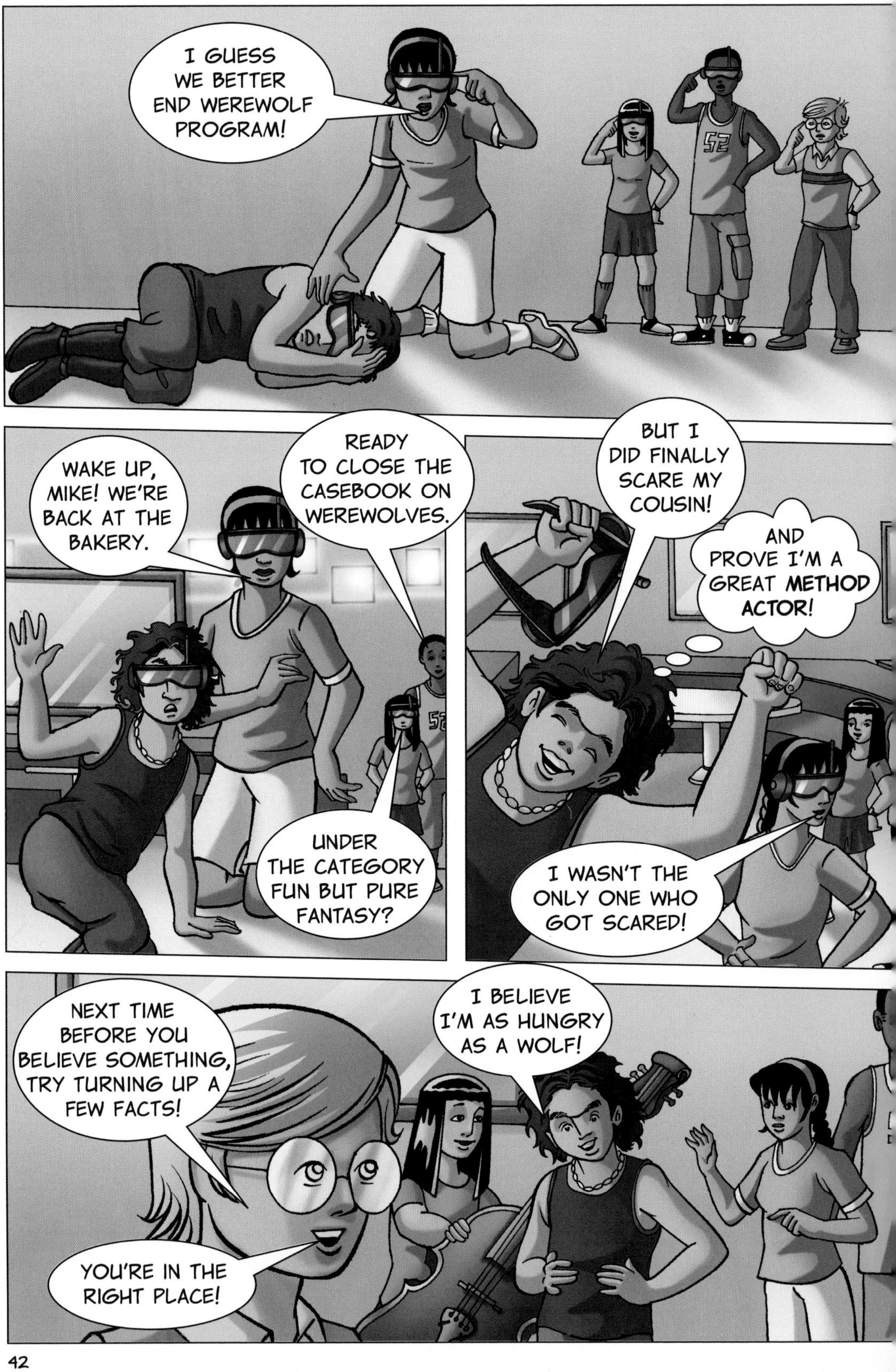
I GUESS WE BETTER END WEREWOLF PROGRAM!
WAKE UP, MIKE! WE'RE BACK AT THE BAKERY.
READY TO CLOSE THE CASEBOOK ON WEREWOLVES.
UNDER THE CATEGORY FUN BUT PURE FANTASY?
BUT I DID FINALLY SCARE MY COUSIN!
AND PROVE I'M A GREAT **METHOD ACTOR**!
I WASN'T THE ONLY ONE WHO GOT SCARED!
NEXT TIME BEFORE YOU BELIEVE SOMETHING, TRY TURNING UP A FEW FACTS!
YOU'RE IN THE RIGHT PLACE!
I BELIEVE I'M AS HUNGRY AS A WOLF!

FACT FILE

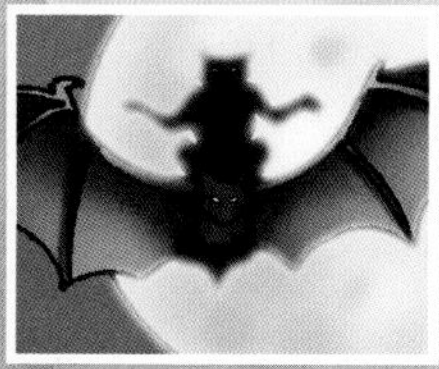

Loup-garou: From the French *loup* meaning "wolf," thought to derive from the exclamation "*Loup, gardez vous*!" meaning "Wolf, watch out!" or literally, "Guard yourself." The type of werewolf described in the folklore from the southeastern United States, populated by the people known as Cajuns. Originally from France, they settled first in Acadia, Maine, and later moved to Louisiana. The Cajuns, as these Acadians came to be known, created their own spicy variations on French culture and cooking—and their own special twist on the werewolf myth.

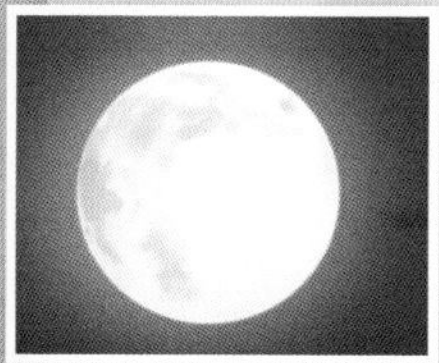

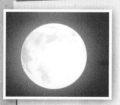

Full moon: The phase of the moon when its full disk is illuminated, so it appears to be a complete circle as opposed to a half, crescent, or sliver. Primitive people had no idea why the moon seemed to change size every month. This "magical" change became linked to other magical changes, like the supposed power to change a man into a wolf.

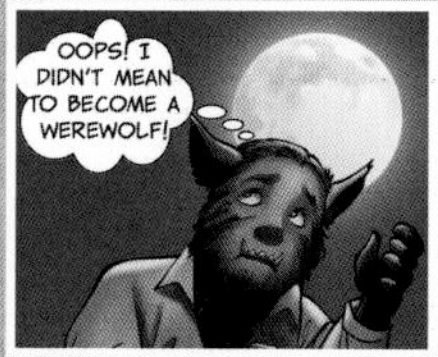
OOPS! I DIDN'T MEAN TO BECOME A WEREWOLF!

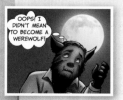

Involuntary: Done without the exercise of the will; unintentional; not under the control of the will; in this case becoming a werewolf through a curse or other misfortune not by performing a magical rite.

FACT FILE

Familiar: In witchcraft, a familiar is a demon in animal form who supposedly serves the witch.

Bayou: Pronounced BY-oo, it's an American French word that comes from the Choktaw word *bayuk*, used to describe the marshy offshoot of a river. In the bayou country of Louisiana, the Cajun werewolf known as the loup-garou supposedly attended dances lively with zydeco music. The muddy bayou and the amazing music are real, but the loup-garou is only a legend.

Druid: An ancient Celtic priest, magician, or soothsayer of Gaul Britain, Ireland, or Wales. (Gaul is the land that is now known as France, before it was conquered by the Franks in the sixth century.)

FACT FILE

 **Repercussion**: An indirect effect or reaction following an event or action; an echo or reverberation; an aftereffect or outcome; a result or consequence. For werewolves, repercussion means that if hurt or killed in wolf form, the human form will suffer the same fate.

 **Serial killer**: A person who murders repeatedly for no apparent reason. An insane person who feels compelled to kill is called a serial killer today, but many of them would have been tried as werewolves in medieval Europe.

 **Method actor**: From the Greek *methodos*, meaning "the pursuit of knowledge," derived from *hodos* meaning "way." In theater, "the Method" refers to a technique of acting based on not just showing but feeling the character's emotions. Method actors find many ways to get deeply into character. Mike's Method acting as a werewolf went a bit too far!

Find Out for Yourself

Wolf cults could fill a different casebook! Find out what the ancient Greeks, Romans, Egyptians, and others believed about wolves and the power of wolves' teeth as charms. Discover the secret Nazi group called Organization Werewolf.

Norse and other myths about shape-shifters could also fill a casebook.

Or learn the other side of the story by finding out how humans hunted wolves almost to extinction!

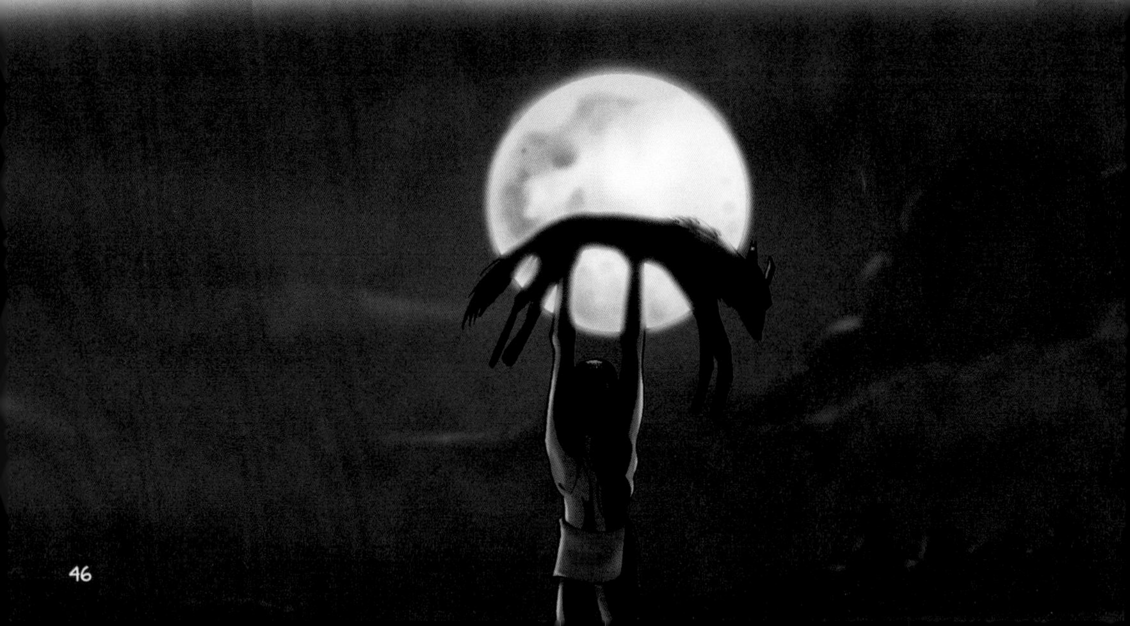

Web Sites

To ensure the currency and safety of recommended Internet links, Windmill maintains and updates an online list of sites related to the subject of this book. To access this list of web sites, please go to

www.windmillbks.com/weblinks

and select this book's title.

About the Author/Artist

Justine and Ron Fontes met at a publishing house in New York City, where he worked for the comic book department and she was an editorial assistant in children's books. Together, they have written over 500 children's books, in every format from board books to historical novels. They live in Maine, where they continue their work in writing and comics and publish a newsletter, *critter news*.

For more great fiction and nonfiction, go to www.windmillbooks.com